Dark Powers

A Decorah Security Novel

By Rebecca York

Ruth Glick writing as Rebecca York

Published by Light Street Press
Copyright © 2012 by Ruth Glick
Cover design by Patricia Rosemoor

This is a work of fiction. Names, characters, places, and
incidents either are the product of the author's imagination
or are used fictitiously, and any resemblance to actual
persons, living or dead, business establishments, events, or
locales is entirely coincidental

ISBN: 978-0-9706293-3-3

CHAPTER ONE

Death or disaster were only seconds away.

Ben Walker leaped from his car, shouting a warning at the slender blond woman crossing the Decorah Security parking lot, oblivious to the battered pickup truck bearing down on her, sun glinting off its windshield.

Dashing into the traffic lane, he snatched her out of the way while the truck rattled past.

The woman he'd pulled to safety clutched his broad shoulders and buried her head against his chest.

While he held her close, he fixed his gaze on the rapidly departing vehicle. It was blue, with no particular distinguishing features except a dent in the left rear bumper. The license plate was smeared with mud. All he could make out was the letter "J" at the beginning.

He kept his arms around the woman, the first female he had reached for in almost a year. The denial of intimacy a punishment for his sins.

She stirred in his embrace.

"You okay?" he asked, hearing the rough quality of his own voice.

"Yes. Sorry. I guess I wasn't paying attention."

"Neither was that bozo. You have any idea who it was?"

She stared in the direction where the truck had disappeared. "No. I didn't even see him."

"The driver was wearing a baseball cap. That's all I could tell."

She made no move to disengage from him, and he liked the feel of her feminine body against his, liked the closeness and the way she put her trust in him.

That thought was followed by the inevitable counterpoint. If she only knew the things he'd done, she would probably leap away—disgusted.

But no more disgusted than he was with himself.

The woman in his arms stirred, snapping his attention back to the present. "Thank you."

"No problem." He cleared his throat. "From where I was standing, it looked like that guy was deliberately trying to run you down."

"I hope not."

When she finally took a step back, he dropped his arms to his sides.

She looked from him to the building in front of them. "You're headed for Decorah Security?

"Yeah." He wondered why she'd questioned him about that. Before he could ask, he realized he'd left the door of his two-year-old Honda wide open. "But I'd better lock my car before I come back and find it missing."

She nodded and headed inside. He returned to his vehicle, locked the door and followed, hurrying to keep from being late for his morning meeting.

When he walked into the plush conference room, the woman he'd snatched from the path of the speeding truck was sitting at the table with his boss, Frank Decorah, a crusty old ex-Navy SEAL who'd gone into the security business after losing a leg in the service. With him was Teddy

2

Granada, one of their IT guys. He was a large man who often forgot to shave and change his clothes but who did fantastic computer work. If the information was on the Web, he'd find it.

"Ben, I'd like you to meet Sage Arnold. She's hired us to find her missing sister," Frank said, then added, "Ben is one of our top agents and the best one for this job."

He let the praise roll off of him. Of course Frank would claim that.

She gave him an anxious look, probably embarrassed by the incident in the parking lot.

Ben managed to say, "Good to meet you."

He had studied the case before coming in, but he hadn't known the woman he'd rescued was their client. She was a hard-working accountant whose sister had gone missing. Frank had taken her case at a reduced rate, as he often did when dealing with distraught relatives of innocent victims. Initially Ben had wanted to turn down the assignment. Then he'd figured that rescuing a woman in pain would be part of his atonement.

"We've contacted the authorities in Doncaster," Frank said as Ben took a seat opposite Sage. "The police chief is certain your sister ran away. Tell us why you think she's been kidnapped."

Ben studied the client. In the parking lot he'd only gotten a quick impression of her. Now he took in her shoulder-length ash-blond hair, her wide blue eyes and her delicate features.

She glanced at Frank, then at Ben and Teddy, before fixing her gaze somewhere in the distance.

"My sister, Laurel Baker, and I are from a family you'd call dysfunctional. We don't have the same name because Mom was married three times. Laurel and I have different fathers, and there was another guy when I was in my teens. Laurel's eighteen, ten years younger than I am, and I've been her role model. One thing I drummed into her was that she'd be stuck in a dead-end life like our mom unless she got a good education. She was working at a restaurant called the Crab Shack in Doncaster part time and going to school at the community college. She didn't come home from the restaurant after her shift a couple of evenings ago."

Ben watched her body language. More than concerned or upset, she seemed ill at ease. Was she lying or simply uncomfortable about speaking so frankly about her family?

Frank said gently, "Chief Judd says there was conflict between her and your mom. Could that have made her leave home? What if she's staying with a friend?"

Sage raised her head and gave Frank a direct look. "If she's staying with a friend, why would that keep her from going to work?"

"I don't know."

The woman dragged in a breath and let it out. "I know something's happened to Laurel. Nothing had changed in her life. There was always some kind of conflict with Mom, but Laurel knew she had to hang in and get her degree. She likes working with people, and she decided to become an X-ray tech because there are lots of good jobs in that field."

Frank reached into his pocket and took out the gold eagle coin he always carried. As he began to turn it over in his hand, he said, "But something could have happened. She could have gotten into drugs. Or even gotten pregnant and been afraid to tell your mother."

"Not Laurel. She's too smart for that."

Ben didn't say he'd thought his own sister, Erin, was too smart to get into the trouble that had killed her, but her story proved that you didn't always know your siblings as well as

4

you thought. Still, for the moment, he'd have to rely on Sage's judgment.

"In our initial phone conversation, you mentioned Laurel's father, Gary Baker. You think he could be involved?" Frank asked.

"Well, after he and my mom broke up, he abducted Laurel."

"Why?" Ben asked. "And when was that?"

Sage sighed. "Eight years ago. My mom was angry when he didn't make child support payments on time. She paid him back by not letting him see Laurel. He's no sweetheart, and he took Laurel away for a long weekend without permission. The authorities gave Laurel back to Mom, of course. But that's part of what I meant about our family problems."

"Did he go to jail?"

"He got probation."

"Your mother was with your dad before she was with Laurel's father?" Frank asked.

"Yes. Married to him. Like I said, I'm ten years older. They eloped when she was seventeen. That marriage didn't last very long. I mean, he left her right after I was born."

"Because?"

"He said I cried too much."

Frank made a snorting sound. "Nice. When's the last time you saw him?"

"Never, really. He disappeared a few years ago, and I haven't made any attempt to get in touch. For all I know, he's in jail or dead. But it doesn't matter what he's doing. He doesn't have anything to do with my life now."

Ben listened to the dispassionate way she spoke, thinking that she had compartmentalized her life. But he knew all too well how that worked.

"You're saying your mother has a rocky reputation with men," Frank said, trying to dig up more insights into the sister's character. "Would Laurel have picked up her mother's habits? Would she go off with some guy she was seeing?"

"No," Sage said emphatically.

They talked for a half hour longer about Laurel and incidents from the past. When Frank was finally out of questions, Ben jumped in.

"I can pay Laurel's father a visit in Baltimore and see if she's there," he said. "If not, I'll go down to Doncaster and see what I can turn up."

The town was on Maryland's Eastern Shore, separated from the main part of the state by the Chesapeake Bay.

Before he finished speaking, Sage shook her head. "I'm going with you."

Ben's gaze shot to her. "It's better if I handle this on my own."

"I'm going."

"It could be dangerous. That attempted hit and run in the parking lot could be connected."

"What hit and run?" Frank asked.

"A pickup almost ran her over."

"I understand someone may not want me poking around this case, but I also know you'll have a better chance of finding Laurel with me along," Sage answered.

"Because?"

"Starting with Gary Baker. I know how he'll react. And if my sister's not at his house, I can help you in Doncaster. I grew up there. In fact when I was a teenager, my circumstances were a lot like Laurel's are now. I worked at some of the local restaurants while I was going to school. I know the community. Doncaster's a tourist town." She glanced at Frank. "You already said the police chief thinks

Laurel ran away. That's because it's the best interpretation he can put on it."

"Meaning what?" Ben asked.

"Meaning that the power structure in Doncaster wants to make sure nothing interferes with the town's income."

"You mean the police chief would hush up a crime to keep the tourists coming?"

"If the town fathers wanted him to do it—and he thought he could get away with it."

"Hard to believe," Ben muttered.

"You'll see what I mean when we get there. It's not like living in the Baltimore-Washington corridor. It's isolated. Insular. And dependent for its prosperity on people who see it as a charming place to visit and spend money."

Ben kept his voice hard, trying to sound discouraging. "I'll have a better chance of finding your sister if I don't have to babysit you." It wasn't what he was really thinking, but he chose that way to express his negativity.

As he'd assumed, her reaction was equally negative. "You won't have to babysit me," she snapped.

The next comment she made was addressed to Frank and a surprise to Ben. He'd been trying to get her to back off. Instead she asked, "Are you sure this is the best man for the job?"

Frank kept his voice even in the face of the obvious animosity between client and agent. "Absolutely. He has special skills that will be invaluable."

"Like what?"

Frank began flipping the gold eagle coin again. "That's information that we only give out on a need-to-know basis."

"I need to know," she said.

"I'm sorry," Frank answered, still playing with the coin. "You'll have to take my word for it."

She scraped back her chair and stood. "I guess I came to the wrong security company."

Ben debated for a moment. It was tempting to let her walk out, and it was also tempting to see her reaction if he shared his secret.

He glanced at Frank who nodded almost imperceptibly. Keeping his voice even, Ben said, "I pick up information from dead bodies."

"You mean like on *CSI?* You're a forensics expert?"

"No. I can . . ." He spread his hands. "Listen in on dead people's last memories."

Sage laughed. "You're kidding, right?"

"It's not a joke."

Sage studied him. "What does that mean exactly? Are you claiming to be a medium or something?"

"I'm not claiming anything. As it happens, I died a few years ago, and the emergency room staff brought me back—with a new ability."

She kept staring at him, probably wondering if they were shitting her.

Ben fought not to say anything he'd regret. He wasn't going to defend himself. He had a special talent that he'd acquired the hard way, and Frank had thought it would be a useful tool for a Decorah Security agent. Today he thought it would help in finding Laurel Baker.

Her sister didn't believe he could do it, and right now there was no way to prove it to her.

He let out the breath he'd been holding when she sat back down.

As he wondered why he cared what she thought, she said, "I'll reserve judgment."

He shrugged. In the parking lot, when he'd held her in his arms, he'd been attracted to her. That was before he'd experienced a taste of their working relationship.

Or maybe they'd find Laurel at the father's house, and this would all be over before it started.

Frank pushed back his chair and stood. "Are we set, then?"

"Yes," Sage and Ben answered at the same time, both of them grudgingly.

Ben turned to Teddy. "See if you can dig up any similar cases in Doncaster."

"If they left footprints, I'll find them," he said.

When they were alone, Sage cleared her throat, and Ben tensed, expecting some caustic remark about his detective skills.

Instead, she surprised him by saying, "I'm sorry. We've gotten off on the wrong foot, and it's my fault."

"No problem," he mumbled, thinking of the adage *the customer is always right.* "You're under a lot of stress."

"I'm not usually this uptight. But Laurel is my baby sister, and I'm worried sick about her. It's all I can think about. That's how I almost got run over out there."

"I understand."

She paused for a second and said, "I guess I feel guilty about what's happened to her."

"What do you have to be guilty about?"

"I left Doncaster and moved to Baltimore because I wanted to make a break with small-town life. I tried to keep up the connection with Laurel, but that's hard when you're a couple of hours away. I mean, we did Skype and e-mailed, but it's not the same as living in the same house." She cleared her throat. "It wasn't just leaving Doncaster. I had to get away from Mom, too. So I understand Mr. Decorah's questions about her wanting to leave, but I know she wouldn't just run away."

"Uh huh."

"Did you ever lose anyone you loved?" she asked suddenly.

He reared back. "Did Frank mention something to you?"

"No." Her voice turned anxious. "Did I say the wrong thing again?"

"My sister." He glanced away. "She took a dangerous job, and I couldn't save her life." He knew she was waiting for him to say more, but he wasn't going to get into anything personal.

He looked back at her. "Let's start with Gary Baker and hope we find her there."

Sage followed Ben Walker into the parking lot, wishing they'd gotten off to a better start together. She'd been wound up with her own fears and insecurities, and she'd jumped down his throat. Now she'd have to tread carefully around him, which was too bad because they were going to be stuck with each other for a while if Laurel wasn't at Gary's.

On the other hand, he'd shocked her with that claim about his paranormal abilities. She'd never put much stock in mumbo jumbo. But maybe he thought he had something special. He'd said he'd died. She'd like to ask him about that, or did she really want to know? Maybe it was better to keep their relationship as professional as possible—and reserve judgment on his psychic talents until he proved the claim or not.

Pausing in the early summer warmth, she turned her mind to logistics. "I guess I can leave my car here. Let me get my travel bag."

"You were prepared to go down there?"

"Yes."

His tight nod told her he wasn't looking forward to riding in the same vehicle with her after the way she'd tried to get him kicked off the case.

This time she came to a dead stop and looked both ways before crossing the parking lot. There was no traffic coming and no pickup truck in sight. Quickly she carried her bag to his Honda and put it in the trunk beside his.

While she adjusted her seat belt, he consulted the material he'd scooped up from the passenger seat, and she studied him covertly.

He was a good-looking guy. Tall and dark with a strong jaw and large hands. Under other circumstances she might have let herself speculate about him, but she was too focused on finding Laurel to think about anything else.

"You know where Gary lives?" she asked.

"I've got the address and a GPS." He punched in the address before pulling out of the parking space.

As they headed down Route 1, Sage cleared her throat. "Can I make a suggestion?"

"Sure," he answered, not bothering to sound enthusiastic.

"He might not let us in, but if we get inside, I want to look around for signs of Laurel. You can ask him a bunch of questions. I'll pretend I have to go to the bathroom and do some snooping."

"Okay," he answered, and she took his agreement to be a good sign.

"Are there any places he could hide her?" he asked. "Like a secret room in the basement or something?"

"He loves her. He had a bedroom all fixed for her when she was allowed to visit. He wouldn't put her somewhere uncomfortable."

"How does she feel about him?"

11

"She hasn't seen him in years. My mom kind of turned her against him."

"So if she acted hostile, he might restrain her?"

Sage thought about that. "I hope not. But he can be violent and impulsive."

"Great. Would he kidnap Laurel to get back at her mother?"

"After all these years? Not unless something had happened that I don't know about." She waited a beat before saying, "Just try not to provoke him."

CHAPTER TWO

Laurel Baker said a little prayer.

"Please, God, let this be a nightmare. Let me wake up and find out I'm home in my own bed."

Of course, when she opened her eyes, nothing had changed. She was in the same place where she'd awakened yesterday with a headache and a foul taste in her mouth. It was a frilly princess bedroom with a pink bedspread, gauzy pink curtains, tons of fluffy pillows, a fairy-tale castle painted on one wall, and a collection of dolls on the shelves of a hutch. An environment that any little girl would love. With the emphasis on *little*.

It was hardly the kind of room eighteen-year-old Laurel would have chosen.

And no way would she have elected to find a manacle around her right ankle—attached to a chain bolted to a metal plate that was secured to the wall.

She could only move so far from the bed—like over to the covered bucket that she was supposed to use as a toilet. A jarring intrusion in this prissy room.

She clenched her teeth, got up awkwardly and crossed to the bucket where she peed and put the cover back. The stuff in there was starting to smell, and she hoped the guy would empty it soon.

Well, that would mean she'd have to see him again, but she was pretty sure she didn't have any choice about that. He'd be coming back, and she'd better be ready to face him.

Face.

She couldn't hold back a mirthless laugh. She couldn't see his damn face because he was wearing a black hood over his head, with small circles cut for his eyes and mouth.

But maybe it was better that she couldn't see his features. If she couldn't tell anyone who he was, maybe he wouldn't have to kill her.

She made a moaning sound and wrapped her arms around her shoulders, rocking back and forth. Several minutes passed before she was sure she wasn't going to start crying. Would he see her cry?

Once again she scanned the room. As far as she could tell, there were no cameras watching, but she was no expert on video surveillance.

The last thing she remembered before waking up here was finishing her shift at the Crab Shack. She'd gone outside and started walking toward her bike, and somebody had come up behind her and clamped a wet rag over her nose and mouth.

She'd dropped like a stone. The next thing she knew, she was here.

She touched her hair. It should be light brown, but she'd seen in the mirror over the dresser that he'd dyed it blond. And dressed her in a frilly little girl's dress that matched the room.

Again she fought tears. At least he hadn't raped her. She prayed it wasn't sex that he wanted. Unless he was into having sex with children.

Another thought circled in her mind. Was he hiding his identity because she knew him? Like could he possibly be her father? He'd kidnapped her a long time ago, and Mom had gotten her back. Had he decided to do it again? She hadn't seen him in eight years. Would she even know him if she fell over him?

As they approached Gary Baker's house, Ben heard Sage drag in a breath and let it out before saying, "Can I ask you a question?"

Wondering what was coming, he kept his eyes fixed on the road. "Okay."

"You said you got impressions from dead people."

"And you think that's a bunch of crap?"

"No," she answered, and he thought the denial was probably reflexive.

The inquiry came in a rush. "What I want to know is—did Frank Decorah send you because he thinks Laurel is dead?"

He heard the fear in her voice and made his answer gentle.

"No. He sent me because he thinks the same thing might have happened to another girl—or girls. And if I find their bodies, I might be able to see the murderer."

"Oh." She took a moment to digest that, then hit him with another question. "You said you died. How?"

He clamped his hands on the steering wheel, then forced himself to relax his grip. He didn't want to talk about himself, but it was a question he'd ask if the shoe were on the other foot.

"I was a police detective in Baltimore. Working narcotics. We raided a warehouse, and I got shot in the chest. I was dead before they got me to Union Memorial."

"Did you see that bright light they talk about?"

15

"I didn't get that far. It was like I was hovering above my body, looking down at the doctor and nurses working on me."

She nodded. "And when you recovered, you went from the police force to Decorah?"

He turned his head toward her briefly before returning his attention to the road. "I spent four months in rehab. I was ready to go back to the Baltimore PD when my sister disappeared."

"Like Laurel?"

"No. It was work related. She ended up dead, and I ended up hunting down the man who was responsible for her death."

"I'm sorry."

He answered with a little nod, wishing she'd get off the subject.

Instead she asked, "You were close to her?"

"We saw each other when we could. . ." He felt his throat tighten. "But she wouldn't listen to me when I told her that career choice was a dumb idea."

"Maybe if you'd put it differently."

"Maybe."

He hoped the flat tone of his voice made it clear he didn't want to discuss it further.

She pressed her lips together. Probably she had other questions, but she was smart enough to keep them to herself now. They had reached Gary Baker's neighborhood, a community of red-brick ranchers built in the fifties, where most of the properties were reasonably well taken care of.

As they turned onto Baker's street, he started scanning for the house. It was the place with the out-of-control shrubbery. The wood trim was in need of painting, the garden was weedy and the grass looked like it hadn't seen a lawnmower in months. The neighbors must love this guy.

"You just passed it," she said, pointing across the street as Ben drove down the block.

"I know. I'm taking the lay of the land before we get out."

"Oh. Sorry."

He glanced at her again, watching her twist her hands together in her lap. Obviously she wasn't looking forward to seeing Baker again.

"He works in a warehouse, right?" Ben asked.

"Last I knew."

"That's what his dossier says."

"You already investigated him?"

"Ted—that's the IT guy—started on him first."

Ben turned the car around so that the house was now on the right. "When's the last time you were here?"

"I visited with Laurel a few times when I was a kid. I remember a standard layout. Living room-dining room combination right off the front door. Kitchen looking over the backyard." She made a snorting sound. "If you think the front looks bad, the back is a junk heap. Or it was. Inside there are three bedrooms, a powder room and a full bath."

"And a basement?"

"Yes. The door's in the kitchen."

"Walk out?"

She hesitated. "I don't think so."

He pulled to the curb. "You think seeing you will make him angry?"

"Hard to tell with Gary. When he's provoked, he's got a temper, that's for sure."

He turned to her. "And you want to take a chance on sneaking around his house?"

Her voice took on a tone of steel. "I have to."

* * * * * * *

17

Sage prepared herself as they both climbed out of the car into the afternoon sunshine and walked up three cracked steps to the front door. The closer they got to the house, the faster her heart pounded.

She hadn't seen Gary Baker in years, and she'd hoped never to see him again. Now here she was—because she was willing to brave any situation if it might help her find Laurel.

When Ben rang the bell, her tension jolted up a notch. After half a minute had ticked by and nothing happened, he rang again.

Finally, she heard noises inside and braced herself. What was Gary doing in there? Locking up Laurel?

The door opened, and the man she hadn't seen since her childhood appeared, looking at least twenty years older than when they'd last met. His dark hair was shot with gray and thinning, and the lines on his face had carved themselves deeply into his skin. She wouldn't have taken him for the vain type, but he'd combed long strands across his balding dome.

His eyes were the pale blue she remembered. His nose looked larger and redder, making her wonder if he'd been drinking a lot over the years. Probably he was in his mid-fifties. And although his face showed his age, his body seemed fit and muscular. Sage remembered that he'd had a gym membership. It looked like he'd kept it up.

His main focus was on Ben. Then his gaze shifted to her, and he did a double take as he realized who she was.

"Sage?"

"Yes."

"What are you doing here?"

"We've come to ask for your help," Ben said, surprising her with the way he'd put it.

"With what?"

"Laurel is missing, and we're wondering if you have any idea where she went."

"Laurel? Missing?" he repeated. If he'd been aware of it before, he was doing an excellent job of sounding shocked.

"Can we come in?" Ben asked.

Gary hesitated, then stepped back. They followed him into a living room that hadn't changed much since Sage had been there in her teens. Well, the clunky old television set had been replaced by a big new flat screen that dominated the wall across from the sofa. Unlike the exterior, the interior was relatively neat. No dirty dishes or papers lying around.

Gary didn't ask them to sit down on the lumpy brown couch. Instead he stood in the middle of the living room with his beefy arms folded across his chest. A defensive posture.

"What happened to Laurel?" he asked.

"We don't know," Sage said. "She left work a couple of nights ago at the restaurant where she's a waitress in Doncaster and never came home."

"You have any idea where she might have gone?" Ben asked.

"No."

"She didn't call or anything?"

"No." Gary swung his gaze to Sage. "What's your involvement?"

"I'm worried about my sister."

"When's the last time you saw her?" Ben asked.

"Eight years ago," he answered as though he'd been keeping track. He gave a mirthless laugh. "Her mom's name is Angel, but she's a bitch on wheels. She never let me near my own kid. For spite, because she sure didn't love hanging out with her daughters."

The remark cut. Sage could think of a couple of snappy comebacks, but she bit them back.

As Ben asked another question, she shifted her weight from one foot to the other. "Do you mind if I use your bathroom?"

He gave her a considering look. "Okay."

Ben walked over to the fireplace where there were some framed photographs. "This is Laurel?" he asked, as he pointed to a picture of a little girl with Gary.

"Yeah. She's the angel. Not her mom."

Sage headed down the hall. Walking past the bathroom, she started opening doors and looking into rooms. She stopped short, her breath catching when she came across an eerie sight—a room with a pink bedspread and curtains that looked like it belonged to a little girl. It was the room she remembered from when she'd visited years ago. And it was still here, as if Laurel had walked out of it only a few moments ago.

It seemed to be empty, but she stepped inside, checked the closet, looked under the bed. The spread was neatly in place, and when she pulled it back, she found that the sheets were crisp.

The room appeared to be a shrine to Laurel, not a place where she'd been living recently.

Sage stepped into the hall again and opened another door. The room beyond looked to be Gary's, with a queen-sized bed, heavy wood furniture, and a carpet in tones of brown and gray.

The third bedroom had been converted into an office.

Down the hall she heard Ben talking to Gary, explaining that Decorah Security had been hired to look for Laurel. He was going into the background of the agency, explaining that Frank Decorah had several offices around the country, but the headquarters was in Beltsville.

Sage paused in the doorway to the living room, noting that Ben had turned so that Gary's back was to her. Slipping past, she headed for the kitchen. The basement door was where she'd remembered it. She opened it quickly, eased inside and felt for a light switch.

After flipping it on, she tiptoed down the stairs, feeling the temperature drop as she descended.

The stairs opened into an old-fashioned pine-paneled rec room that smelled vaguely musty. At the far end was another door. She opened it and saw the furnace room. As she crossed the tile floor again, from above her she heard Gary shout, "Hey, what's going on?"

"Nothing," Ben answered.

"Where is Sage?"

Footsteps pounded down the hall, then came back. Gary had obviously discovered that she wasn't where she'd said she'd be.

She was on her way back up when he charged into the kitchen, spotted her on the stairs and yanked her up into the room, where she stood wavering on her feet.

"What the hell are you doing?" he shouted at her.

"Nothing."

"Don't tell me nothing. You were spying on me."

"I wanted to make sure Laurel wasn't here."

Ben was right behind him. "Get off of her."

Gary whirled around and slammed a beefy fist toward Ben. He dodged aside and tried to defend himself without fighting back. Probably he figured that the guy had a right to be pissed off that they'd lied their way into his house.

"Meet me outside," he shouted to Sage, but his attention had swung away from Gary for a split second too long. The man grabbed a frying pan off the stove and brought it down on Ben's head.

He staggered back, then slid down the wall, landing on his butt on the kitchen floor, looking dazed.

"Ben!" she shouted, but he didn't answer.

With his opponent out of the way, Gary turned toward her.

"Are you lying about Laurel? Did you use that excuse to get in here?"

"Why would I do that?"

"You tell me, honey."

"We're only looking for my sister. You have to admit that if you kidnapped her once, you might do it again."

He made a dismissive sound as he advanced on her. "I see you inherited your values from your mom. Well, I'm going to teach you a lesson you won't forget."

Sage was already sure she wasn't going to forget this incident, but right now she had to get out of here and dial 911. She feinted to the left, then right when he grabbed for her. Ducking around him, she charged into the living room and made it halfway across. Before she could reach the door, he caught up with her, grabbing her by the hair and yanking hard enough to snap her head back.

As she gasped from the sharp pain, he spun her around and flattened her against the wall, his face inches from hers. The murderous look in his eyes made her throat close.

She tried to raise her knee and slam him in the groin, but he was ready for the move.

"No, you don't."

He swept her legs out from under her with his foot so that he was the only thing holding her up.

As she dangled in his clutches, he pulled her toward him, getting ready to slam her head against the wall. Before he could do it, Ben staggered out of the kitchen, blood running down his face. He was holding the same pan that Gary had

22

hit him with. Coming up behind the man, he slammed it onto his head.

Gary let go of Sage and went down. Pressing her shoulders against the wall, she struggled to stay on her feet, wondering how everything had turned deadly so quickly.

"Come on," Ben said, grabbing her hand and pulling her across the living room. As they charged outside, he slammed the front door behind them.

Blinking in the sunlight, Sage thought they were going to make a clean getaway. Well, as clean as you could expect with blood dripping down Ben's forehead.

They were almost to his Honda when the door behind them opened again, and Gary's voice rang out.

"Stop right there, or I'll shoot."

They both whirled around to see Baker standing on the porch, holding a gun. And Sage knew he was fool enough to use it.

CHAPTER THREE

"Get in the car," Ben said as he pulled an automatic from the back waistband of his slacks.

There was no way Sage was going to obey that order. She was rooted to the spot where she stood, as she watched the two armed men facing each other in the hot sun like a scene out of a western.

One of them had a volatile streak as wide as the Chesapeake Bay. She wasn't sure about the other one yet.

"It's against the law to fire a weapon in a residential area," Ben said.

"Then why do you have a gun in your hand?" Baker challenged.

"To keep you from doing something stupid."

As they confronted each other, a couple of doors along the street opened.

Gary stood his ground for another moment, then with a curse, he turned and stalked back into his house, slamming the door behind him.

Ben waited until the other man had disappeared, then headed for the car.

"Wait," Sage called to him.

"Why?"

"Your head's bleeding."

"Head wounds do that. We'll take care of it after we get out of here."

Sage followed and got into the passenger seat as he slid behind the wheel and started the engine with a jerky motion, then lurched away from the curb.

"This is a bad idea," she said. "Pull over. I'll drive."

"Not yet."

He kept going, and she wondered if the blow to the head really had addled his brain. Could he even see with blood dripping in his eyes?

But after a few blocks, he came to a gas station and pulled in, driving around back to the men's room.

"I'll be right back," he said as he got out. At least he seemed steady on his feet as he went inside. When he came back several minutes later, he'd cleaned up his face, and he was holding a wad of wet paper towels to the top of his head.

"Let me see."

He sat down in the seat, with his legs dangling out of the car, leaning forward slightly. She came around to his side of the vehicle and lifted the paper towels away.

"Well?" he asked.

"It's pretty deep."

He grunted.

She gently dabbed at the wound. It felt intimate, touching him like this, as intimate as when he'd held her in the parking lot. Then she hadn't known who he was. Now she was getting a much better picture of Ben Walker.

Well, sort of. They'd been together a few hours, and he had revealed only a little about his background, with her working to get at the information. She knew he'd cared about his sister and lost her. That made her feel closer to him.

And she knew more, from their interaction and from observing him. He wasn't afraid of a fight, or a gun battle, or of taking chances. She didn't know what would have happened if Gary hadn't backed down, but she was glad she hadn't had to find out.

At first he'd tried not to injure Gary, then he'd gotten conked over the head defending her. All that told her that he had a strong sense of right and wrong, which didn't necessarily dovetail with conventional morality. Probably he'd known that searching Gary Baker's house was a dangerous idea, but he'd gone along with her plan because it was the quickest way to make sure Laurel wasn't there.

"I'm sorry you got hurt," she murmured.

"How bad is it?"

"The cut's about three quarters of an inch long. I don't want to poke too much and start it bleeding again."

"Sounds like it's not too serious."

"Did you lose consciousness?"

"No. I just got knocked on my ass."

"You need to put antiseptic on it."

"I have a first-aid kit in the glove compartment."

She climbed back in the passenger seat, pulled out the kit and looked inside. The antiseptic was in a square packet which she tore open. From behind him, she pressed the pad to the wound.

He winced.

"Sorry."

"Not your fault."

Technically, it was. The whole thing.

She repressed the impulse to stroke his cheek. He was wounded on her account. But there couldn't be anything personal between them. This was strictly a business arrangement, and when they'd found Laurel, they'd go their separate ways.

"Do you think he'll call the cops?" she asked.

Ben made a snorting sound. "Not likely. A guy with his temper probably has a rap sheet. Or at least complaints from the neighbors. My guess is that he won't want anything to do with the authorities."

"A neighbor could call it in."

"Then let's hope nobody got our license number." Changing the subject, he said, "What did you find in there while you were poking around?"

"He's kept Laurel's room the way it was when she was a little girl. Like a shrine."

"Obsessive." He paused. "And sad."

She hadn't thought of him as sad, but the description fit.

"But I didn't see any signs that she was actually in the house."

"How far did you get in your search?"

"I looked in all the bedrooms. Then I went downstairs into the rec room. From there to the laundry room. She wasn't in any of those places. And I don't think he'd put her in the attic in this weather. He loves her, and it's like an oven up there."

"Then our next stop is Doncaster." He turned to her. "You're sure you want to come?"

"Yes," she answered immediately. "And I'll drive."

She felt his hesitation. He was probably the kind of macho guy who didn't let a woman behind the wheel of his car. But in this case, his better judgment prevailed.

"Okay."

They both got out and exchanged places.

"You know how to get there from here?" he asked.

"Yes. Head for Annapolis, then the Bay Bridge."

Under other circumstances, she might have told him to take a nap. But he'd been hit on the head, and there was some chance he could have a concussion.

To keep him engaged, she said, "I told you a little about Doncaster," she said. "I can give you some more background."

"Sure."

"It's on a fairly wide peninsula between the Chesapeake Bay and the Atlantic Ocean, with a lot of rivers running through the area. Because it was the closest part of the U.S. to England, and the rivers made transportation easy, it was settled early. The British saw that the area was important and tried to invade during the War of 1812, but the Americans beat them off.

"It was kind of downhill from there. What made it prominent early on worked against it later. It was cut off from the mainland, and until the 1950s when the Bay Bridge was built, you had to take a ferry to get across. A lot of people made their living fishing, crabbing, oystering. As the water quality of the bay declined, so did those industries. Now they've got big chicken farms and some agriculture. But the same factors that kept down the population have also worked in its favor. It's a quaint area that still has a lot of eighteenth-century charm. Particularly since the Bay Bridge was built, the main industry is tourism. It's the lifeblood of Doncaster, and they have to make the bulk of their money in the warmer months, which is why the power structure is so protective of the town's reputation."

The man next to her didn't comment.

"Ben?"

His eyes snapped open. "Sorry."

"I'm putting you to sleep." Just the opposite of what she'd intended.

"No. I was listening."

To make sure he wasn't concussed, she asked him a question. "Are we on the Eastern Shore or the Western?" she asked.

He hesitated for a minute. "Western."

"How do you know?"

"It's hard not to notice a bridge that's over four miles long."

She laughed. And in fact, they came to the toll booth a few miles later and crossed the high span to Kent Island, then continued down Route 50 to Doncaster.

As they approached, Sage felt her stomach muscles clench. When she'd been a young girl, she'd loved living in such a cute little town. Later, she'd felt the undercurrents of tension below the surface. That was one of the reasons she'd left. Her mother was another. Angel Baker simply didn't have Sage's values. As soon as she'd been able to make it on her own, Sage had fled. At first she'd shared an apartment with a friend who'd moved to Baltimore to work for the Social Security Administration. Then she'd been able to afford her own small apartment in the less gentrified part of Catonsville.

Leaving Laurel in Doncaster, she reminded herself. She hadn't been back here since Laurel's birthday six months ago. She'd intended to visit her sister, but she'd kept putting it off with one excuse after the other.

Now it might be too late.

She forced back a sob as her hands clenched the wheel. It wasn't too late. Laurel was still alive. She had to be, and they'd find her before anything bad happened. She shuddered as her mind suddenly bombarded her with unwelcome scenarios. Rape and murder for starters.

When she glanced at Ben, she saw him watching her. "It's going to be okay," he said.

She hadn't expected reassurances from him, and his words brought tears to her eyes.

"Thanks," she whispered, unable to speak any louder past the knot in her throat.

They drove down Main Street past tee shirt and craft shops, restaurants and real estate offices. The sidewalks were crowded with men, women and kids in vacation attire, some carrying shopping bags.

Ben turned his head toward a family of four, all licking giant ice cream cones. "I see what you mean about it being a tourist town."

"There are beaches all along the river. And it's only a short drive to the bay. The ocean's still forty minutes away," she answered, glad to focus on something besides her own guilt.

"Give me the lay of the land."

"Like how?"

"Drive down the street again. Tell me who owns the businesses and if the owners are part of the power structure."

At the end of the commercial area, she turned into the Methodist Church's parking lot and came back, driving more slowly this time.

When they passed the hardware store, she said, "Craig Fellows has been in the hardware business here since before I was born, and he inherited the store from his dad. It's an essential part of the community. And he's one of the wheeler-dealers in town."

She pointed toward the bank. "The bank president, Martin Kendley, is also a power in town. He and William

Hinton have traded places as mayor a few times. Hinton's got it now."

"What does Hinton do?"

"He's a developer. And another one of his pals is George Myers. He owns Pine Fairways, a golf course and resort just down the road from downtown."

They passed a couple of real estate offices. "Phil Davis handles high-end properties."

"No women are part of the power structure?"

"I guess Doris Jenkins, the owner of several clothing boutiques, would qualify."

"Any of the people you mentioned ever been involved in shady stuff?"

"If they had been, the police chief covered it up."

"There's only so much he can do if a crime is on record." Ben waited a beat before asking, "Where were you planning to stay? Not with your mom, I assume."

"Lord no. We're coming up to several motels."

"Pick one."

"We're getting two rooms," she blurted before she thought about how that sounded.

"Of course," he answered.

The first few motels they passed were full. The third, a place called the Beach Breeze, was more than she wanted to spend, but she had the feeling they weren't going to do any better.

She and Ben both went into the office and got adjoining rooms facing the highway.

They each stowed their luggage and took a few minutes to freshen up, then met back at the car.

"I'd like to talk to my mother," Sage said. "Well, that's actually not the way I'd put it. But I want to watch her face when she tells me what happened to Laurel."

"You think she'd lie to you?"

"Or not tell everything she knows. Unless she thinks it's to her advantage."

"Okay. We can put her first on our agenda. Then the police. Then the Crab Shack." He gingerly touched the top of his head. "I can drive."

She didn't argue because she sensed he hated being a passenger in his own car.

"Left or right?" he asked as he turned the car toward the highway.

"Left. It's not far."

They headed for the other side of town, to the modest bungalow where Sage had grown up. It was on a side street that ended abruptly in a swampy area.

The house had once been painted white. Now it was fading to weather-worn gray. The boxwood hedge around the front yard hid a patch of dirt and straggly weeds. The property had been part of Angel Baker's divorce settlement from Gary Baker.

Ben made no comment as he followed her up the sagging steps to the front door. She still had a key in her purse, but she knocked and waited until her mom answered the door.

She'd been hoping for the best. But when Angel Baker came to the door, Sage was embarrassed.

Her mother, who was in her mid-fifties with graying hair dyed blond, had on too much lipstick that was three shades too dark for her pale complexion. Her dress was a tight-fitting green number. And her high heels would have broken Sage's arches.

Mom didn't say hello when she saw her older daughter standing in the doorway. Instead she greeted her with, "I was just getting ready to go to work."

"We'll only keep you a minute," Sage said, wishing she'd asked Ben to wait in the car.

"Good because I've only got a minute."

"I came down here looking for Laurel. Aren't you worried about her?"

"I'm worried about keeping my job, so I can pay the bills."

As a salesclerk at one of the shops in town, Sage assumed. She didn't know which one because Angel had been fired from a number of positions. She claimed that migraine headaches sometimes laid her low. Sage understood that was code for hangover, but in the tourist season, the shopkeepers needed clerks who knew how to use a computerized cash register, and they were often willing to give Angel Baker the benefit of the doubt.

"When was the last time you saw Laurel?" she asked, keeping her gaze on her mother's face.

"I already told you over the phone when I checked to see if she'd gone to your place. Two days ago, when she left for the Crab Shack. She never came home that night."

"Her bed wasn't slept in?"

"No."

"Were any of her clothes missing?"

"I don't know."

"And you called the police?"

"Not till the next afternoon."

"Why did you wait so long?"

"I expected her to come home. And when I talked to Police Chief Judd, he said she probably ran away."

"You believe him?"

"I don't know what to think. That girl and I were rubbing each other the wrong way something fierce."

Sage could understand why. That was exactly her reaction every time she came home.

Angel had switched her focus to Ben, looking him up and down with an appraising eye like she was considering trying to get him into her bed. "You going to introduce me to your friend?"

He answered, "I'm Ben Walker from Decorah Security."

"Which is?"

"A detective agency," Sage answered. "I hired them to help me find Laurel."

"A detective agency with a fancy name," Angel said. "Are they expensive?"

"You don't have to worry about that," Sage snapped.

"And Laurel hasn't been to work since two nights ago?" Ben asked.

"As far as I know."

"Any thoughts about where she might have gone?"

"She got friendly with some of those waitresses that live down at Mrs. Borden's. She could have crashed with them."

"A motel?" Ben asked.

"A boarding house where women live who are working here for the season," Sage answered. "Some of them are from Baltimore. Others are from out of the country.

"Yeah, they jabber in languages you can't understand," Angel added, making Sage cringe again. It was a long time since she'd interacted with Angel in the presence of anyone besides Laurel. It wasn't pleasant imagining what Ben must think.

"We'll check there," Ben said as he kept his gaze on Angel. "Can we have a look at Laurel's room?"

"I'm on my way out."

"I've got the key," Sage answered.

Angel eyed Ben. "I don't like having strange men in the house," Angel answered.

Sage could think of a cutting retort about the strange men she'd tripped over in the morning. Before she could say anything, though, Ben answered, "We'll be out of here in no time."

Angel grudgingly stepped aside, and Sage led Ben toward the back of the house, trying to see the interior from his point of view.

Angel had a bohemian style and a knack for working with other people's cast-offs. An old chair was artfully draped with scarves. The sagging sofa was disguised with a comforter. And Sage remembered when her mother had dragged home the throw rug she'd found outside someone's house on trash day. Of course, it had taken a couple of treatments to get the cat pee smell out, but now it was a colorful addition to the room.

Sage led Ben down the hall to Laurel's room, which was quite different from the little girl's room at Gary Baker's.

"We used to share this room," Sage said. "But when I moved out, she took it over."

There were still two beds, covered with light blue spreads. One looked like someone had climbed out of it and pulled up the covers in a hasty attempt to smooth them out. The other was piled with stuffed animals that Laurel had collected over the years. Bears, cats, a moose and even a couple of wolves.

A dresser held a jumble of cosmetics and stands with earrings and bracelets. The walls were decorated with posters of hot male rock singers. And when Sage opened the closet, she found blouses, blazers, jeans and a few skirts on hangers, and more clothing lying in a pile on the floor.

"If she ran away, it doesn't look like she took her clothes," Ben commented.

"Or her makeup or jewelry," Sage added.

She crossed to the bed with the stuffed animals and picked up a brown bear wearing a cheerleader's uniform and carrying pom-poms.

"I gave this to her when she made the cheerleading squad in high school. She loved it. I don't think she would have just left it here if she was planning to take off."

"Yeah," Ben agreed.

He opened some of the dresser drawers and looked under tee shirts and shorts.

"What are you doing?"

"Checking for drugs."

"She doesn't use them."

"As far as you know."

She glared at him. "She wouldn't."

He closed the drawer and went on to another. "We need to be objective."

She wanted to say that was easier for him than it was for her. Instead she kept silent.

He felt under the mattress and came out with a flat cosmetic bag.

Sage watched him open it. Inside was seventy-five dollars.

"It must be from her pay," Sage said. "And she sure wouldn't leave that."

"Right."

When he started to put the money back, Sage reached for the bag. "I'll keep it. In case Mom decides to do some snooping."

He glanced toward the door. "You think she'd take it?"

"I wouldn't put it past her."

Sage put the money in her shoulder bag.

When they walked back to the front of the house, they found that Angel had already left.

Sage locked the door behind them, then climbed into the car, keeping her gaze straight ahead.

"Mom wasn't always that bad," she said defensively as they headed back to the car.

"What happened?"

"She's had a hard life. She'd like to be dependent on a man, but the relationships never work out."

"Why?"

"She's no judge of character. If a guy is halfway nice to her, she gets too friendly, and they take advantage of her . . . availability. When they get to know each other better, the relationship is likely to blow up in her face."

"And she took out her frustrations on you and your sister?"

"I wouldn't put it quite so strongly. When I was little, she used to try harder with us."

Ben said nothing, and Sage felt even more uncomfortable..

"I should have left you back at the Beach Breeze."

"No. I need to get the whole picture, and she's part of it."

CHAPTER FOUR

Ben kept his tone neutral. He knew Sage had been embarrassed by the encounter with her mother, but he wasn't going to tell her she shouldn't have come to Doncaster.

He hadn't been prepared to partner with her, but he was starting to see how she'd be an asset to the investigation.

"Police station next," he said.

"It's one street over from Main. On Oyster. Next to the new library building."

He headed for Main. After turning the corner, he glanced in his rearview mirror and spotted a blue pickup truck behind them. An ordinary model. There must be scores of them in Doncaster, but this looked like the one that had almost run over Sage in the parking lot at Decorah Security. When he slowed down, trying to get a look at the driver in the rearview mirror, it sped around him and barreled down Main.

He sped up.

"What are you doing?" Sage asked.

"Up ahead. That looks a lot like the pickup from the Decorah Security lot. The one that almost ran you down. There's mud on the license plate, like this morning. And the driver's got a baseball cap pulled down over his face."

She peered through the windshield at the vehicle. "I didn't get a good look when I was at Decorah. Just a flash of something blue bearing down on me. There's a 'J' on the license plate. That's all I can see under the mud. And the right rear bumper is dented."

"Sounds like our suspect, but I didn't spot him on the way to your mom's." He tried to catch up, but the light changed, and the truck zipped across. He could almost imagine the guy in the cab giving them the finger.

"Maybe it was a coincidence."

"Maybe," he answered, but in his experience, what looked like a coincidence often turned out to be just the opposite.

When the light changed, he drove several more blocks through the shopping area, but the vehicle in question had disappeared. And there were too many tourists on the street for reckless driving.

"He's gone," Sage murmured.

"Yeah." Ben turned to look at her. "Did anyone know you were going to Decorah Security?"

"I didn't tell anyone."

"And I guess from your mom's reaction, she didn't know."

"I figured—why bother."

He thought over her answer. "Did you spot the truck on the way over to our offices?"

"I was preoccupied."

He nodded. Someone could have followed her from her house.

"We were going to the police station."

"Right. Which way?"

"We have to turn around."

She told him the cross street, and he doubled back, turning then turning again onto Oyster and pulling up at the police station. It was in a converted clapboard house with a wide front porch. The lawn had been replaced by a wide blacktop parking lot—with a prominent sign marking the Chief's space. A new Ford King Ranch pickup truck was parked in the slot. A model he knew started around fifty thousand dollars. An expensive ride for a small-town police chief.

He switched his attention from the chief's wheels to the quaint station house. The facility was probably from about the same era as Angel Baker's house, but in far better repair.

"Looks charming, but I guess they've got jail cells in there."

"I've never been inside. The station used to be in a modern building on Main—totally out of keeping with the rest of the area, but they got a deal on this place. Probably Phil Davis handled the transaction, with the other guys I mentioned chipping in some of the cash—above what the town had to pay. Phil got to move his real estate office to the old building and added some charm to the exterior. Charm is important in Doncaster."

"I'm beginning to realize that," he said dryly. "And connections."

When Ben didn't get out immediately, she gave him a questioning look.

"I'm thinking about our approach."

"Which is?"

"I think we'll tell him the same thing we told your mom. The truth. You've hired Decorah Security to help you find your sister."

When she looked uncertain, he asked, "What don't you like about that?"

"I told you that the town wants to avoid trouble. Judd won't like it if he thinks we're pressuring him."

"If we don't tell him I'm from Decorah and he finds out later, that might make things worse. Or maybe he already knows. I mean, how did that truck show up outside our offices? It sounds like someone was sent to stop you from investigating your sister's disappearance."

She winced. "I hate to think someone would actually come after me."

"Do you have a better explanation?"

"I wish I did."

"Let me do the talking."

She bristled. "Because?"

"Just from the little you've said, you've given me the impression that the chief is more likely to deal with a man on an equal basis than a woman."

"He's not likely to deal with anyone on an equal basis, except for people like the mayor and the bank president."

"That bad?"

"They pay him, so he's respectful. Otherwise he considers himself a step above ordinary mortals."

"I'll keep that in mind."

They climbed out of the car, and Ben looked around, noting the cameras mounted along the roof line.

"Don't do anything you don't want recorded," he murmured as she followed his gaze.

The Victorian charm ended at the door. Inside, the building had been completely remodeled with a high desk separating the waiting area from the offices in back. A young, uniformed officer standing behind the desk looked at them inquiringly as they stepped through the front door. His blond hair was cut short, and his uniform was neatly pressed. He appeared to be the kind of guy who thought the uniform set him apart—perhaps following the chief's example. Ben had known men like that in other assignments. This guy's name tag said "Lancaster."

In response to the officer's stare, he said, "We'd like to talk to Chief Judd about Laurel Baker."

"The girl who ran away?"

"The girl who's missing."

"And you are?"

"I'm Ben Walker from Decorah Security." He got out his P.I. credentials and put them on the desk.

Lancaster inspected the creds and pushed them back toward Ben. "I'll see if the chief is in," he said.

Ben refrained from pointing out that if the chief wasn't in, someone was using his parking space.

They waited at the counter, saying nothing. Finally the kid came back, followed by a heavyset man with a stomach that would have earned him a trip to the diet doctor in a metropolitan police department. But this was the Eastern Shore of Maryland, Ben reminded himself, where the rules were apparently more lax, at least in regard to physical fitness.

The chief's thinning hair was cut short. His eyes were close-set and steely. And his ears looked like they'd been taped back to hold them next to his head.

"I'm Chief Judd," he said, glancing at Sage before addressing Ben.

"Pleased to meet you. Ben Walker from Decorah Security."

"Which is located where?"

"Between DC and Baltimore."

"What brings you all the way over here?"

He refrained from pointing out that he'd already told that to the desk officer. "We're trying to get a line on Laurel Baker who didn't come home from work two nights ago and hasn't shown up since."

"Runaway most likely."

Beside him, Ben could see Sage reacting. "She didn't run away," she blurted. "She had no reason to run away. She was in school, and she had a job working at the Crab Shack."

"And you are?"

"Her sister."

"Your mother is Angel Baker?"

"Yes."

"And your name is?"

"Sage Arnold."

"I'm guessing you don't know that your mother came to the Crab Shack two days ago to speak to Laurel?"

"No. About what?"

"They were having a right good argument. Your mother was yelling at her that she was working too many hours and letting her grades slip, and she'd better shape up or ship out. She yelled back that if that was what your mom wanted, she didn't have to live there anymore."

Sage looked shocked. "People heard all that?"

"Well, I got it from Bettie Henderson, the restaurant hostess. She heard the whole thing."

Sage nodded numbly, and Ben wondered if her assessment of her sister's disappearance had been all wrong. Yet there was something about the smug expression on the chief's face that set Ben's teeth on edge. The man looked like a master chess player who'd just checkmated his opponent. Which made him wonder if Chief Judd really believed Laurel had run away or if he was more interested in a quick solution to the problem.

"Let us know if you get any more information," Ben said.

"Of course," the chief answered, his tone upbeat. "Where can I contact you?"

He handed over a card with his cell number.

Judd studied the card. "You got a local address?"

"You can get me on my cell."

"You going back to Beltsville tonight?"

"We don't have firm plans," Ben answered, continuing with his evasive answers.

"I wouldn't want you to waste any more of your time. If she wants to be found, she will be."

"You're sure it's not a kidnapping?" Ben asked.

"We have no evidence of that."

Beside him Ben could almost feel Sage vibrating with the need to speak. Before she could, he took her arm and led her outside. The minute they stepped onto the porch, she opened her mouth, but he tightened his grip on her, and she got the hint.

She gave him a quick look, then nodded.

As soon as they got into the car and closed the doors, she turned to him.

"My mother lied to us! She said that the last time she saw Laura was when she left for work."

"Maybe she felt bad about her part in Laurel's disappearance."

"Or she knew I'd get mad when I found out. All she cares about is herself."

"She did call to ask if Laurel had shown up at your house."

She sighed.

"In any case, I'm not going to take the chief's word for the shouting match at the Crab Shack. He looked pretty pleased with himself when he gave us the information."

"I didn't notice."

"You were upset."

She nodded and said, "I want to go over there now."

"Agreed. Where is it? I didn't see it on Main Street."

"It's one block closer to the town dock."

"You know Bettie Henderson?"

"I don't think we ever met. I guess she moved to town after I'd already left."

They retraced the route to the main drag, and he found a parking space in one of the many lots designed to make shopping easy for tourists. The restaurant, a large building of weathered wood, was on the harbor side of the street, with a bank of windows looking out over the moored boats. There was a private dock where patrons who came by water could tie up. As Ben and Sage walked toward the door, seagulls wheeled overhead.

"A prime location," he said.

"It's been here since before I was born. The ownership changed about twenty years ago."

"You really are up on local history."

"In Doncaster, everyone knows everyone else's business. The guy who used to own the restaurant killed his wife."

Ben winced. "I guess they couldn't cover that up."

"I guess not. Because of the scandal, the current owner got it cheap."

They stepped inside. The interior continued the nautical theme with captain's chairs, fishnets and floats on the wood-paneled walls. There were also pictures of Doncaster in the late nineteenth and early twentieth centuries.

The dinner hour was just starting. A slender, efficient woman with short-cropped dark hair was seating a pair of customers. When she came back to the podium, she looked at Ben and Sage.

"I still have some nice tables available by the window."

Ben hesitated. He hadn't come here intending to actually have a meal, but it struck him that both he and Sage had missed lunch. "Yes, that would be great," he answered.

Sage gave him a confused look.

As the hostess led the way to the table he said in a low voice, "We do need to eat dinner."

"Yes, but . . ."

"This gives us a chance to judge the atmosphere here."

The hostess turned toward them. "Something wrong?"

"Not at all," Ben answered.

They sat down and waited until the woman had left.

Ben leaned toward Sage. "I know you're anxious to find Laurel."

"And I feel like we're wasting time. We could grab hamburgers from a fast-food place if you're hungry."

"We could, but this is a working dinner."

Just then the waitress approached their table. Her name tag said "Sonja."

"Can I get you something to drink?" she asked.

He caught her accent and smiled. "Where are you from?"

"The Czech Republic."

"That's interesting. Your English is very good."

"Thank you."

"How did you happen to end up in Doncaster?"

"There are companies that hire women to work in the United States. You must have good English skills to get accepted."

"Are most of the waitresses here part of the program?"

"About half of us."

"Do you know Laurel Baker?"

Her expression changed. "Why do you ask?"

"I'm her sister," Sage blurted. "We're trying to find her."

The woman's gaze swung toward her, and a look of sympathy crossed her face, but her words didn't match her expression. "I have to get back to work. I'm sorry. Did you want something to drink?"

46

Ben chose a beer from a local brewery. Sage opted for iced tea.

When the waitress had left, she leaned across the table and said with exasperation in her voice, "We didn't learn much."

"Quite the contrary."

CHAPTER FIVE

Ben kept his own voice even. "We know that a lot of the waitresses are from out of the country. And we know that Sonja is reluctant to talk to us about Laurel."

"She could be reluctant to slow up her waitress duties."

"Is that what you really think?"

"No," she admitted.

He could see other diners looking at them, particularly a casually dressed, gray-haired man and woman. Were they locals who might know something about Laurel? Or tourists who had picked up on the conversation?

Sonja came back with their drinks, looking wary. "Are you ready to order?" she asked.

"Sorry," Ben apologized. "We haven't really looked at the menu."

"A lot of people like the crab cakes. Or the crab imperial. Or the crab-stuffed rockfish."

He laughed. "Well, this is the Crab Shack." They both ordered the shellfish specialties, and Ben added a side order of onion rings.

Ben took a swallow of his beer. He didn't usually drink on the job, but he figured one beer wasn't going to blur his judgment. While they were waiting for their dinners to arrive, the hostess came over, looking slightly wary.

"I overheard you talking to Sonja about Laurel," she said. "I'm Bettie Henderson."

After the introductions Ben said, "I hope we didn't get Sonja in trouble."

"Of course not. And there's nothing she can tell you about the night Mrs. Baker came here because she wasn't on duty."

"But you were?"

"Yes."

"Can you tell us about it?"

She looked uncomfortable. "I don't like spreading gossip."

"I need to know what happened," Sage said.

Bettie gave her a sympathetic look. "All right. Laurel had taken some extra hours, and apparently her mother wasn't happy about that."

"Why not?" Sage asked.

"She said that Laurel was letting her grades slip."

"I can't believe that's true," Sage answered.

"I guess you'd have to ask her professors at the college."

"Yes, if they're not going to claim the information is confidential," she answered.

"Was Laurel having any problems at work?" Ben asked. "Apart from her mother showing up to castigate her in public."

"She wasn't having any problems here. She was a good worker. She got along with the other girls."

"Anything you can tell us that might point to a reason why she could have run away?"

She thought for a moment. "If I had to name anything, it would be her relationship with her mother."

"She talked to you about that?" Sage asked.

49

"All of the girls know they can come to me with their personal concerns."

"Has anyone else on the staff run away or disappeared?"

Bettie Henderson hesitated, then said, "I'd like to say no, but I'm sure you'll find that two other girls went missing. One six months ago and the other about a year ago."

"Who?"

"Two of the guest workers."

"Did they find out what happened to them?"

"I don't think so, but they could have thought that working in this country gave them an opportunity to disappear into the American landscape."

"Maybe. Anything else you can think of that Laurel and her mother said to each other?"

Bettie waited a beat before lowering her voice. "Laurel said that if her mother was going to 'ride her' she could always move out."

"Did she say where?"

"No."

Before Ben could ask another question, their meal arrived.

"I should let you eat."

"If you think of anything, please call," Ben said, handing her a card.

She stuck it into a pocket of her lavender shirtwaist, then went back to the podium.

Ben began to eat, finding he was hungry. "This is good."

Sage made a sound of agreement, but he saw that she was less enthusiastic about her crab cakes.

"You should eat."

"I know."

She forked up some more of the crab cakes, then took one of the onion rings.

50

Frank had brought it up earlier, but now that they were in town, Ben asked, "Does Laurel have any friends she could move in with?"

"I don't know." Sage thought for a minute. "And if she did, wouldn't she still be going to work?"

"I'd assume so. Unless there's something going on we don't know about."

They ate the rest of the meal in silence.

When Sonja came back to clear their plates, he told her they didn't want dessert. "Just the check, please."

"Certainly," she said, and he had the impression she was glad to see them leave.

As he paid the check with a credit card, Ben noticed the older couple was still looking at them.

"It's too late to do any more poking around," he said. "We'll start again in the morning."

"I want to go back to my mother's."

"And accuse her of lying?"

"I won't put it that way, exactly," Sage answered, but he wondered what she would do in the heat of the moment.

Police chief Everett Judd drove several hundred yards down a gravel road that led to a vacant house. He cut the engine, turned off his lights, and waited in the darkness under the shade of an old maple tree. He didn't like being ordered to a meeting at the pleasure of the two men who had summoned him, but he'd gotten himself into this situation, and he didn't see an easy way out.

They'd lived in Doncaster all their lives. He'd moved here after answering an ad for a police chief. The community had seemed like a good place to settle down. A backwater where his duties wouldn't be too taxing, and the job had come with the hint of extra income.

For a few years, he'd been happy with the arrangement. Lately, he'd been thinking about moving on. If that was still possible.

And would anywhere else be better than Doncaster?

He'd asked himself that question a lot recently.

After a few minutes, he glanced at his watch in annoyance. The two men who paid him a lot of cash under the table were late. The bastards were usually late, maybe because they wanted to make it clear who had the upper hand.

Judd would like to leave and let the latecomers stew in their own juices, but he knew that wasn't really a good idea.

When he finally heard the sound of another vehicle crunching down the road, some of the tension eased out of his chest. Still he waited with his hand on his gun until he made out the shape of the Mercedes SUV approaching. A Mercedes SUV. What a dumb idea, but he guessed that a guy with money to throw around could get anything he wanted.

The vehicle turned around and pulled up so that the two cars were positioned with their drivers' windows facing each other.

It was dark inside the other car, but Judd could easily picture the two men. Both in their fifties. Both too caught up in the elevated lifestyles they'd come to enjoy. And both drunk on the power they wielded in town. Big fish in a small pond who were sure they had a good thing going.

When the driver rolled down his window, Judd did the same and got a blast of expensive cigar smoke along with warm night air.

No hello or nice to see you. The meeting started with a question. "Where are they now?"

No need to ask who the question referred to.

"At dinner." He cleared his throat. "My guy says they spotted him tailing them."

The driver answered with a string of curses. "He's the one who went up to Beltsville?"

"Yeah."

"You don't have anyone better?"

"He's okay. It's just that the detective with her, Ben Walker, is sharp."

"You have plans for them this evening?" the driver demanded.

"Uh huh. Some pointed discouragement."

"Well, use a different vehicle."

"I plan to." He cleared his throat. "The woman's not going to just walk away without looking for her sister."

"You have any idea where the little bitch went? If we could just find her—dead or alive—that would solve all our problems. I mean, if she's dead, couldn't it be from a drug overdose or something? That could happen anywhere."

Judd winced. These guys were extending themselves beyond his wildest imaginings. But one thing he knew for sure: They weren't paying him enough to cover up murders. Didn't they know the medical examiner in Baltimore would determine the cause of death?

For the moment, he only said, "I don't have anything on her so far. What about your sources?"

"If somebody we know has her, they're not saying."

The other man in the SUV made an angry sound. "This is just what we need right now."

"The group will back us, 'cause they're scared of bad publicity."

"That only goes so far," Judd answered.

"I'd like to find that damn girl, strangle her myself and leave her beside the highway for her nosy sister to find," the car's passenger growled.

"Do you know where the sister and the detective are staying?" the driver asked.

"Not yet. I tried to get him to tell me, but he only gave me his card—with his cell number."

"Just great." The man started his engine and roared away, leaving his cloud of cigar smoke behind him.

Cursing, Judd closed his window. There was something going on in Doncaster that he didn't know about. Something these guys didn't know about either. Unless they were lying to him.

As they were leaving the Crab Shack, Ben noticed that the older couple was hurrying to follow. As he and Sage stepped outside into the twilight, Ben gave them a chance to catch up.

The gray-haired woman approached him. "I couldn't help overhearing you talking about that girl who works here."

"Laurel Baker?" he asked.

"Yes." She looked like she was about to say something when a dark-colored sedan pulled across the parking lot and sat with its engine idling nearby. The woman's husband hurried over, took her by the arm and steered her away from Ben and Sage. He watched them climb into their car and drive away as the sedan continued to idle nearby.

Sage glanced at him, then pressed her lips together as they walked to his car and got in. When the door was shut, she finally spoke.

"That woman was going to tell you something."

"Looked like it."

She turned around and stared at the car that was still in the parking lot. "And she decided it wasn't a good idea."

"I'd like to know why your sister's disappearance is such a big deal in Doncaster."

"You think there's some kind of conspiracy?"

"I don't know. But we're going to find out what's going on," he said, hearing the determination in his own voice. He'd come down here thinking that maybe Laurel *had* run away. Now he was sure there was more going on. Was she involved in something bad? He hoped not, for Sage's sake.

He tried to get a look at the license plate, but the light was out, and like with the pickup truck, the numbers and letters were obscured by dirt.

As they drove out of the restaurant parking lot, he said, "Show me where the rich people in town live."

"There are a lot of estates along the river. And some new developments. One is at Pine Fairways."

Sage directed him to the river road and pointed out the estates where William Hinton, the mayor, and Martin Kendley, the bank president, lived.

"There's so much planting, you can't see their houses," Ben commented.

"I guess they like their privacy. But we can get a good look at Chief Judd's house."

She directed him to a less prestigious but still pricey area of town. The chief lived in a bungalow that had been recently updated with new siding and a large detached garage. The lot was large, with plenty of trees and lawn.

"I'd say he's living above his means," Ben said. "With that new siding and his fancy truck. It would be interesting to know where he gets the money and if he paid taxes on it."

Their next sightseeing tour was to the golf course, where large houses had been built on well-tended lots along the edges of the fairways.

"George Myers, the owner, lives here, of course," Sage said, pointing to a beige brick Tudor. "And Phil Davis who sold most of the lots is also here. He still has a financial interest in the development."

As they continued their tour, they picked up a tail. This time it was a white jeep with a yellow dome light on top. A security vehicle.

"This place is well patrolled," Ben said.

"I guess it's part of the membership fee."

When they exited the golf course and turned back toward their motel, a big sedan appeared in back of them and stayed there.

As they hit a deserted stretch of road, the other car sped up so that the headlights behind them were almost blinding.

Sage twisted around in her seat, then straightened again, a look of panic on her face. "What are they doing?"

"Riding our bumper."

Driving fast on the dark, narrow road wasn't smart but Ben had no choice when the car behind them edged up closer.

The other vehicle was larger and more solidly built than Ben's Honda, and it began pushing them toward the side of the road where only a narrow shoulder separated them from a swampy area.

The road curved, and Ben fought to stay on the blacktop, but the other car wasn't giving him much room, and his right wheels hit the shoulder. The vehicle began bucking on the uneven surface, then skidded, heading toward the swamp.

CHAPTER SIX

"I put my gun in the glove compartment," Ben shouted to Sage as he pulled the car out of the skid and back on the roadway.

"What?"

"My gun. Get it."

She opened the glove compartment and took out the Sig he'd pulled at Gary's, holding it like it might be a live grenade.

He snapped his attention back to driving as the big sedan once again zoomed up and forced them off the road. If they hit the swamp they'd be sitting ducks.

From the other direction, headlights of oncoming cars illuminated the game of tag. It wasn't just one vehicle coming toward them but a string of them, all in an excellent position to witness the scene on Ben's side of the road.

It was enough to give the driver of the sedan second thoughts. Instead of forcing them into the swamp, the other car dropped back and finally turned onto a side road before disappearing from view.

Ben let out the breath he'd been holding and eased back

onto the shoulder, then stopped the car and cut the engine.

Lifting the gun from Sage's hand, he put it in the door compartment beside him.

"What was the gun for?" she asked.

"I didn't know what they had planned if they'd driven us into the swamp."

She winced. When he didn't start the car again, she asked, "What are we doing now?"

"That shoulder was pretty rough. I want to check the tires."

When he turned toward the door, her hand shot out and clamped on his arm. "This is a dangerous place to get out of the car. I mean, they could come back. Or someone coming in our direction could hit you in the dark."

He reconsidered. "Yeah."

She leaned across the console toward him, and it felt natural to reach for her. As soon as he touched her, he felt her shaking.

When he pulled her toward him, she sighed and came into his arms, holding tightly to him.

"I'm sorry," she breathed as he pulled her to him.

"For what?"

"For the way this is turning out. I dragged you into something I didn't understand. In a few hours with me, you've been hit over the head, had a gun pointed at you, and almost been run off the road."

"None of that is your fault," he answered, stroking his hands over her back and shoulders, feeling the tension in her muscles.

"I just thought I was looking for my sister. I didn't know that we were going to be stirring up . . . I don't know what."

"Not your fault," he said again.

Her voice hardened. "If they think they're going to drive

me away, they've got it backwards. This is just making me more determined to find out what happened to Laurel."

"Agreed."

She made no move to leave the shelter of his arms. He'd liked the feel of her in his embrace the first time he'd held her. He liked it even more now that he knew her better. It was almost beyond temptation to tip her face up and bring his lips down on hers, but he fought the impulse because getting personally involved with her wasn't part of his assignment. He had a job to do, and when it was completed, they'd part ways. That was the best thing for her.

"Okay?" he asked.

"Better, at least."

He eased away from her, and she leaned back into her seat.

After starting the engine and waiting for a car to pass, he pulled onto the blacktop, heading in the direction of the Beach Breeze, glad it was dark because he didn't want Sage to see the grim expression on his face. This assignment was shaping up a lot differently than he'd anticipated. In more ways than just having her along.

It had been touch and go there for a few minutes. The big car would have driven them into the swamp if the traffic hadn't come along, providing a bunch of witnesses to the scene.

Beside him Sage sat absolutely still. When he drove past the motel, she jerked toward him. "What are you doing?"

"Making sure they're not on our tail again."

"And then what?"

"I'll turn around and go back."

"You think they don't know where we're staying?"

"If not, I'm sure they can find out," he answered, glad that he had the gun.

59

"Who are they?"

"I'd like to know. Best I can say is somebody with a vested interest in driving us out of Doncaster."

"Just because of my sister?"

"I don't know, but our asking questions about Laurel obviously touched a nerve."

He continued several miles closer to town, then used a gas station to turn around.

A few minutes later, he pulled into the motel parking lot and stopped in front of his door.

Cutting the engine, he cleared his throat. "I know we got separate rooms, but there are two beds in each of them."

"And?"

"And I don't want you spending the night alone after what just happened."

She hesitated for long moments.

"It's safer to stay together, and I'm not going to come on to you, if that's what you're worried about," he added, thinking that the statement might be more convincing if she hadn't ended up in his arms a few minutes ago.

"All right."

He released a pent-up breath, glad that she hadn't put up a substantial argument.

"Stay in the car until I check the rooms," he said.

After she gave him her key, he retrieved the gun and held it down beside his leg as he climbed out of the car and looked around before approaching his room.

Sage stayed in the passenger seat while he unlocked the door and stepped cautiously inside. He checked the closet and the bathroom. No one was inside and, as far as he could tell, no one had disturbed the room or his luggage.

He repeated the procedure with her room. After he'd brought her bag over to his room, he motioned for Sage to follow him. She came inside, then sat down stiffly in one of the chairs at the round table under the window.

Ben laid the gun on the table and sat down in the other chair, then got out his Smartphone and began to send a text message.

"What are you doing?"

"Asking Teddy Granada at Decorah Security if he can confirm the information about the other two missing girls and give us their names. Then I want to know if he can find any others. And I'd like to know about any other crimes that might be relevant."

"Like what?"

"Murders. Kidnappings."

Sage grimaced.

After he sent the message, he decided to get comfortable, so he got out his laptop, then pulled back the spread on one of the beds, kicked off his shoes and propped up a couple of pillows. He laid his gun on the bedside table and sat down with the computer.

Sage kept her gaze on him. "And now?"

"I'm writing a report to Frank Decorah, detailing the scope of what we've encountered down here. Starting with the incident at Gary Baker's house."

Sage watched him typing, his keyboard skills economical and efficient. Like the way he'd held the gun—which he kept within easy reach. He seemed equally at ease with the laptop and with the firearm.

"You think the guys in the car are coming here?" she asked.

"No."

"Why not?"

"For one thing, this room is close to the highway. And

61

someone might see them if they tried to break in. Also, the road incident may have convinced them that a blunt-force assault isn't the way to go."

"I hope you're right."

"I'm a light sleeper. And the gun's right here."

When he finished the report, he stayed on the Web.

"What are you doing now?"

"Looking up Chief Judd."

"And?"

"He's in his mid-forties. Been in town for five years. He's divorced. His two kids live with his ex in Raleigh where he was a patrol officer."

"How did he get to be chief here?"

"It's not an elected position. The mayor and council choose the chief. I guess they were looking for someone with his qualifications."

"Which are?"

"Adequate police experience and a guy willing to be accommodating. Including looking the other way when it's expedient."

"How do you ask about that in a job interview?"

"You don't. You have to take the measure of the man," he said, thinking about what he'd conveyed when he'd applied for a job on the *Windward*, the ship where his sister had been murdered.

"Sounds charming," Sage answered, and he applied the sarcastic comment to both himself and Judd.

"He probably keeps the town safe for tourists and residents."

"Unless you happen to be a girl who gets kidnapped," Sage muttered.

Or gets herself into something unsavory, Ben silently added, because he wasn't going to torment Sage with that observation. He still didn't know what was going on here, and he had to keep all possibilities open.

At eleven they turned on the local news, but there was nothing relevant.

"It's like Laurel doesn't exist," Sage muttered when the newscast concluded. "I mean, when women go missing, aren't there usually big news stories?"

"Your mom isn't making a big deal of it, and the cops are treating it as a runaway."

"I could do a big interview with a TV reporter. They're always looking for news. They'd be glad to get the story from the worried sister's point of view."

"I wouldn't advise it. Better to keep a low profile while we're investigating."

Her frustration made her argue. "We're not that low a profile. We got noticed as soon as we got to town. According to you, *before* we got to town."

"We've got to consider what we gain and what we lose by going public. Don't you think a media circus might detract from the investigation?"

"It would add a sense of urgency," she shot back. "That older woman at the Crab Shack wanted to tell us something. Maybe she'd come forward."

"Or maybe she'd be even more afraid." He gave her a direct look. "And you have to consider that we might scare the kidnapper. Suppose he kills Laurel *because* we went to the media."

She sucked in a quick breath. "I didn't think about that."

"It's a possibility."

"You're thinking a couple of steps ahead of me," she admitted in a low voice.

"It's my job. In the morning, we'll think about our next move." He looked across at her. "You should go to bed."

63

"What about you?"

"I'll stay up for a while. If they're going to attack us here, the most likely time is around two in the morning."

"Why?"

"That's when people are at their most vulnerable. It's probably something to do with biorhythms. Plus, there are fewer witnesses. I'll get some sleep after three. You should go to bed now."

"I can't sleep."

"You may be surprised."

Laurel tensed as she heard the sound of a car pulling up outside the house where she was being held. Taking her lower lip between her teeth, she put down the book she'd been trying to read. A Nancy Drew mystery that she'd enjoyed years ago. Like the other books in this frilly room, it was for a kid. But it was better than having nothing to occupy her mind.

Straining her ears, she heard a door opening. Footsteps. He was home. Walking around the house, getting ready to come back to her. He stayed away for long periods. Because he was at work, she guessed. Now he was off.

Of course, she couldn't be sure what time it was. Night, she thought, judging from the lack of light peeking in through a crack in the boards covering the only window in the room.

He didn't come right to her room. Because he wanted to make her suffer with anticipation? she wondered. Or because he was putting on that spooky costume he always wore when he came to her?

The man who was about to put on a black hood stood in front of the mirror trembling with anticipation—and uncertainty. He'd already put on the black shirt and slacks. The black shoes. His gloves were on the edge of the sink. And the black hood itself. With a hand that wasn't quite steady, he fingered the material, feeling the soft texture. He didn't really want to wear it, but it was necessary. At least for now, until Wendy could accept him for what he was.

He ran shaky fingers through his hair, combing it back from his face. He pressed his hand against the top of his head, trying to hold onto the here and now, but his vision blurred and his mind drifted away.

With a curse, he fought to bring both back into focus.

When he felt steadier, he stared in the mirror, cataloguing his features, zeroing in on eyes that were chocolate brown and worried.

"You're okay," he told himself, then said his name aloud. Another touchstone.

Finally he felt calmer. Everything was as it should be.

Wendy was waiting for him. His pretty little blond daughter. He'd thought he'd lost her, and he'd missed her so much. But he had her back again. Only it wasn't quite right. It was never quite right.

The face in the mirror swam in his vision for a moment, and he squeezed his hands into fists as he fought to hang on to the essence of himself.

His head spun. His mind took gigantic leaps, from the present to the past. Once again the horrible picture surged into his mind. His wife with her hands around Wendy's neck. His panic as he tried to tear her away. Then his sick realization.

Only none of that was real. Not at all. It was only a scary scene he'd made up to terrify himself.

Long seconds passed, and he breathed out a sigh of relief. He was back to normal. He could go in and give his daughter dinner now and spend some quality time with her. She'd be anxious to see him. Even if he still had to wear the hood when he was with her.

The lock turned, and Laurel faced the door, watching as he came in carrying a tray, studying him but trying not to be obvious.

His appearance didn't disappoint her—if that was the right word. He was wearing the same outfit he always wore. Black slacks. A black shirt. Black shoes and a black hood that covered his face, with only holes for his eyes and a slit at his mouth. And leather gloves. She didn't know which was worse, the mask or the gloves. He didn't want her to see his face. And he didn't want to leave fingerprints.

"I brought you dinner, Wendy," he said.

Wendy. Did he have her mixed up with someone else? Should she correct him? She'd considered it. But then she'd thought about how he'd dyed her hair and dressed her up. She must be a character in his fantasy.

"Thank you," she answered. She was hungry, and the aroma of the meal drifted toward her. "It smells good."

"Fried chicken, mashed potatoes, green beans."

"That's very thoughtful of you."

He put the tray on the floor out of her reach, then pushed it forward with a stick. She ordered herself not to move too quickly. Climbing off the bed, she reached for the tray and pulled it the rest of the way toward her, then put it on the bedside table and removed the cover.

The smell of the food overwhelmed her. Picking up a chicken leg, she began to eat.

Her captor sat down in an easy chair across the room, watching her. It made her feel like the act of eating was dirty, but she was too hungry to stop.

When the leg was cleaned of meat, she forked up some mashed potatoes. There was also a can of Coke, which she opened and took a couple of swallows.

"Do you like your room?"

"Yes."

"I hope you're comfortable."

"I'm fine."

"Good."

She kept eating, glancing at him from time to time, trying to figure out what he wanted. There was something weird about him, something she couldn't pinpoint. Maybe about the way he walked or the way he sat in the chair.

He could be nice. Then she'd say something she thought was okay, and he'd start to scream at her, his voice going high pitched and tight.

She wanted to ask his intentions, but she was afraid to be so direct. Was she the first girl who had been in this room? If not, what had happened to the other ones?

"You're very kind to bring me such good food," she said.

"Don't try to say what you think I want to hear."

"What should I say?"

"You'd better figure it out."

While she was eating, he reeled in the slop bucket and set it outside in the hall, then pulled another one from outside and pushed it toward the wall where she could reach it.

"It would be easier to talk if I could see your face," she said, totally reversing what she'd thought about his getup.

"That would ruin everything."

She wanted to ask why. She wanted to find out why she was here. She didn't have the guts to voice the questions. And probably it was dangerous to probe.

"What do you like to do for fun?" he asked.

67

"I don't have much time for fun. I mostly study and work."

"You're a little girl! You don't work."

"Oh. Right." She filed that away for future reference. Little girl. Check.

"What do you like to do?"

Her gaze flicked around the room and landed on the toy shelves. "Play with dolls."

"I got lots of dolls for you."

"Yes. Thanks."

"Are you sure you like the dolls?"

She nodded.

"Which one do you like best?"

She got up and crossed to the shelf, turning her back on him as she studied them. Some were life-sized baby dolls. Others were smaller Barbies. And there were Madame Alexander dolls in elaborate costumes.

"I like the princess one."

"I want to watch you play."

Even as she nodded, she wracked her brain, trying to think about what kind of game he wanted to see.

Feeling awkward, Sage grabbed her overnight bag and took it into the bathroom. She hadn't considered that she might be sleeping in the same room with anyone, so she hadn't brought pajamas. But she did have a long tee shirt that would work.

After taking a quick shower and drying her hair with the dryer provided by the motel, she put her bra back on, along with clean panties and the big tee.

When she came out of the bathroom, Ben was sitting in the same place he'd been before. His gaze flicked to her and then away, and she knew he'd been listening to her getting ready for bed. How could he help it? There was only a thin door between the bedroom and the bathroom.

"How's your head?" she asked.

"Okay."

"You're sure you don't want me to, uh, take guard duty when you go to sleep?"

"I think we'll be okay."

He'd left on the light on the bedside table. She slipped into the bed opposite his and turned away from the light, still feeling his gaze on her. Or was she imagining that?

It had been a long time since she had spent the night with a man. With anyone, for that matter.

He'd said he wouldn't come on to her, but she was all too aware of his masculine presence occupying the bed a few feet away. She had only met him that morning, but they'd been thrown into a pressure cooker together, and the turmoil had driven them closer in ways she didn't want to think about too much.

If she turned would she find him staring at her?

She decided it was better not to find out.

When he got up, she tensed, but he was only going into the bathroom. This time it was her turn to listen as he used the toilet and showered. As he came out again, she watched him through slitted eyes. He had taken off his slacks and was dressed in a dark tee shirt and dark briefs. Apparently he hadn't counted on having a roommate either.

The scent of soap and man drifted toward her as she rolled to her back and tried to do relaxation exercises.

Exhaustion and the nerve-wracking day were catching up with her, and she finally drifted off.

Ben had planned to stay awake, but the blow to his skull had taken too much out of him. Despite his best efforts, he drifted off.

And almost immediately, the dream grabbed him. The one he'd been having for months. The details varied, but the basics were always the same.

He was in a field of straggly weeds that stretched as far as his eye could see. And he walked among the dead. They came toward him, each of them alone. Men and women. Some were recognizable as human beings with pale skin and large, questioning eyes. Others were mere skeletons. And worst of all were the ones that looked like they'd climbed out of a six-month-old grave.

He pressed his palms against his sides, willing them to stay there, but it was impossible to stop from reaching out and touching some of them as they passed, catching their last earthly thoughts before blackness closed in.

Fear. Panic. Sadness. Shock.

A boy dressed in swimming trunks walked toward him with jerky steps. As he passed, Ben touched him and learned he'd dived into the shallow end of a pool and hit his head, water filling his lungs as his paralyzed body refused to respond.

Next was a man in a business suit who had stared at the black hole in the barrel of an automatic pistol before the muzzle flash and a moment of blinding pain.

After him was an eighteen-year-old woman, her thoughts swallowed up by panic as a truck careened toward her car.

And then the worst of all. A slave girl from the *Windward*. She'd called herself Jewel, and he'd never known her real name.

She'd been petite, with olive skin, long dark hair and hazel eyes. Nothing like his sister, yet she'd reminded him of Erin. Naive. Eager for adventure. Eager to please. Ben had found her in one of the dungeon rooms, dead. A man who took pleasure in giving pain had tied her down and tortured her. The guy had crossed the line, and there had been no one to stop him.

Not Ben Walker or anyone else.

In the dream, Jewel's eyes met his. He'd touched her in the morgue. Now she reached out toward him, and he reared back. He didn't want to watch her final moments. Not again.

Somehow he clawed his way out of the dream and lay panting in the bed, his body covered with perspiration.

Glancing over, he was relieved to see that Sage was sleeping. Not watching him relive part of his life that he longed to forget.

He clenched his fists, willing the wisps of the dream from his mind. Sitting up, he pulled off his undershirt and used it to mop the sweat from his face and neck, then tossed the shirt on the bed beside him. He was thinking about getting a drink of water when he heard a noise outside. A car pulling up.

He was off the bed with his gun in his hand before the engine cut off.

Something woke Sage from sleep, and her eyes snapped open. The bedside lamp was off, but dim light filtered in from around the drawn curtains. For a moment she didn't know where she was. Then it all came back to her. Laurel missing. Decorah Security. Ben Walker.

He was standing by the window, wearing only the dark briefs he'd worn to bed, and holding the gun as he pulled the edge of the curtains aside to look out. Tension radiated through his well-muscled body. The muscles of an endurance runner, not a weight lifter.

She sprang out of the bed, and he whirled toward her, the gun pointed in her direction.

CHAPTER SEVEN

Sage froze as she stared down the barrel of the automatic and beyond it to Ben's tense face.

"Christ!" He lowered the weapon. "I'm sorry."

"What happened?"

"I woke up when I heard a car pull into the lot outside. I wanted to make sure it wasn't someone coming after us."

"Who was it?"

He made a dismissive sound. "A man and woman on their way in from a late night."

She shivered in the cold. She'd been staring at the gun. Now she stared at the man, at his well-toned body, his narrow waist, the dark mat of hair that spread across his chest, split by an eight-inch-long scar.

"You should go back to bed," he said.

That was the truth. She should. Instead she walked toward him. He'd said he'd been shot. Thank God he'd recovered.

Reaching out, she wrapped her arms around him and pressed her face against his shoulder.

"Don't." The word was a low rumble in his chest.

"Why not?"

"Because you're in a fragile emotional state, and you're

reacting to danger instead of thinking rationally."

She blew off the flat, emotionless statement. "I've been trying to think rationally ever since Mom called to ask if Laurel was at my house. It's not working. Too much is happening too fast."

"I scared you," he muttered.

"Not you. Everything."

Unable to stop, she pressed against him, warming herself with the heat of his skin.

To her relief, he put down the gun, then lifted his arms and folded her close. One of his large hands played with her hair, combing through the strands. The other stroked her back and shoulders in small circles, working the tight muscles.

He made a muffled sound deep in his chest as he reached down, slipping his hand under the hem of her shirt and sliding it upward, splaying it against the bare skin of her back, sending prickles of heat through her body.

Heat that warmed her from the inside out.

She closed her eyes, wanting to focus only on the man who held her in his arms. Tonight she'd come to him for comfort and discovered she wanted a lot more than that. No, she'd known it when she climbed out of bed, but she hadn't been able to admit it.

When she lifted her head, he went very still.

Reaching up, she clasped the back of his head and brought his mouth down to hers. Their lips met in a kiss that turned hot the moment they touched.

The contact drove all the uncertainty from her mind. She forgot everything but his taste, his touch. And her own out-of-kilter response.

She needed to get closer to him, as close as she possibly could. If she had ever felt such desperation, she could not remember when. All she could do was lean into him, caught by the steamy pleasure of the contact.

"Sage," he murmured against her mouth, nibbling with his lips before settling into a more steady pressure.

She liked the way he kissed and the way he said her name with an edge of the desperation she felt. It made her reckless, made her feel as if she was a prisoner of forces that held her in their grip.

Wrapping her arms around Ben, she felt the hard shaft of his erection between them. When she moved against it, his hands went to her hips, pulling her more tightly to himself.

They rocked in each other's arms, caught in a cloud of sensuality that was carrying them away from this place and time to somewhere better. For heartbeats she thought they were going there together.

Then he shattered the moment as she felt the pressure of his hands against her shoulders, easing her away from him.

His breath shuddered.

Her eyes blinked open, and she stared up at him, struggling with confusion.

"Don't push me away," she managed to say.

"I have to."

"Why?"

"You know this is wrong."

"Why?" she asked again.

"You hired Decorah Security to find your sister—not have me seduce you."

"You weren't seducing me. I was the one who came to you."

"And I should have sent you back to your bed."

He was being too damned rational, but she knew there was no returning to the place where they had been. She stepped away, turning her head, embarrassed that she had pushed the two of them so far when she knew as well as he did that it was the wrong thing to do.

Before he could say anything else, she climbed back into her cold bed and burrowed under the covers, wrapping her arms around her shoulders as she tried to warm herself.

Ben had thought there was no way he could go back to sleep. But perhaps he wanted to get away from the little room where he and Sage were confined, because he drifted off quickly. Yet sleep was a trap, too. When another dream seized him, he tried to fight his way to consciousness, but he couldn't wake. And this time, to his horror, he was back on the *Windward*, walking down long corridors, past closed doors. He knew the passengers were in the rooms beyond the doors, enjoying the pleasures that the slaves provided.

He had always shunned those pleasures, and he had never understood why his sister was turned on by the sexual games she liked to play.

Yet as he walked down the passageway, imagining what might be going on in those rooms, he could feel his body responding. Finally he paused in front of one of the doors. He told himself he didn't want to go in, but he knew that was a lie.

He turned the door handle and walked into the chamber beyond. It was a dungeon, like something out of a medieval castle. Although the lighting was low, he could clearly see the walls that looked like stone, the racks of implements, a wooden table with restraints for hands and feet, the large X-shaped wooden beams against one wall with hand and foot manacles attached.

He wanted to feel disgust when he looked at the room and the equipment, but a surge of sexual excitement coursed through him. It ramped up when he saw Sage standing in the room, a satisfied expression on her face. She was dressed as he had never expected to see her—like a dominatrix in black leather shorts, a low-cut leather vest, black fishnet stockings and black high-heeled shoes. The effect was bold and sexy.

She watched him taking in her appearance.

Giving him a considering look as he stood by the door, she said, "I'm glad you've finally arrived."

"I don't want to be here."

"Why not?"

"I don't want to participate in any of this stuff."

"Not even when you need to be punished?"

"For what?"

"You're the one who thinks you deserve the punishment. For being the security chief here. For letting people die on your watch."

"I . . ."

"Take off your clothes," she said in a harsh voice. "Or get out of here, and never try to contact me again."

Her words made his heart stop, then start to pound in double time. Never see her again? That was unthinkable.

With hands he couldn't quite hold steady, he pulled the knit shirt he was wearing over his head and tossed it onto the chair in the corner. Then he began to unbuckle his belt. He unzipped his jeans and shucked them down his legs. Now he was wearing only the briefs he'd had on in the motel room.

"Take them off," she said in a sharp voice.

He was aroused, and the idea of facing her that way, in this room, embarrassed him. But he had no choice. Not anymore. He pulled off the briefs, feeling his cock spring free.

She ran her eyes up and down his body, fixing on his erection. Stepping forward, she took him in her hand, weighing him, caressing him lightly, her touch jolting up his sexual need.

"Are you ready to take your punishment?"

"Yes," he managed to say.

She looked around the room, considering. "I could have you against the wall, but I think I like the table better. Lie down on your stomach."

He did as she asked, his breath hissing in and out of his lungs as he lay on the uncomfortable wooden surface while she secured his wrists to leather thongs at the top corners of the table, then his ankles to the bottom.

Walking along the length of the table. She stroked his butt and ran her hand between his legs to squeeze his balls. Then she reached under the table and opened a trapdoor so that his cock and balls were exposed. She reached through the opening, stroking his penis, drawing a gasp from him.

He was so hard he thought he would climax right then, but she leaned down, her lips close to his ear and whispered, "You had better not let yourself go. That's part of your punishment."

She walked away from him, and with his head turned to the side, he could see her standing beside the wall of implements.

When she turned back to him, she was holding a short whip with several braided leather strands. "I think we'll use this."

She slapped them down on his back several times with small, stinging strokes. Then she moved down to his ass, striking him over and over, making his flesh burn and his cock swell with blood.

When she stopped, his whole body was tingling.

"I need to come," he panted.

"Not now. Not until I give you permission."

"When?"

"When you're ready to accept yourself."

* * * * * * *

Sage woke to the sound of the shower running. Ben must be getting dressed, which gave her a little time to collect herself before she had to face him.

He was right. She'd been off balance and swept up by emotions last night. Worse, she'd made a fool of herself. And worse still, she'd been behaving the way her mother always did.

What had she said to him about Angel Baker? That she wanted to be dependent on men? And what had Sage done last night but demonstrate the same behavior?

She made a disgusted sound, wishing she could be out of the room before he got out of the bathroom. But then what? They only had one car—his car—and she wasn't planning to hike into town. Angry with herself, she pawed through her bag, looking for clean clothes to wear, wondering what the heck they were going to say to each other when he finally came out.

Ben finished drying himself. Finished pulling on his clothes. Finished shaving. Each thing he did was slow and deliberate, because he didn't want to open the damn door and face Sage. Not after that dream.

Only she hadn't been in the dream, he reminded himself. It had been his imagination. He'd put himself back on the *Windward* and put her there with him.

He wasn't sure what it meant. He'd hated the place. He'd thought he had participated in evil there.

Yet going into that dungeon with her had turned him on. What she'd done to him had turned him on more. Thinking about it was turning him on now, and he deliberately forced himself to calm down.

He didn't like the implications of the dream. But there was nothing he could do about it now.

78

He took a deep breath and opened the door.

Sage looked at him, then away, and he knew she was thinking about the scene between them. The real scene. Not the one his unconscious mind had conjured up after he'd sent her back to bed.

He focused on keeping his breath even as he stepped back into the bedroom.

"I think we should separate today," Sage said.

Had he heard her right? And what was he going to say?

As he shaved, Everett Judd stared at himself in the bathroom mirror. Turning his head one way and then the other, he inspected his sagging jowls. He should be drinking less beer and exercising more, but three or four cans of brew in the evening were the only way he could cope with life in Doncaster. That was better than the hard stuff, he rationalized. As for exercise, by the time he finished putting in a day at the police station, plus the other duties assigned to him, he was too tired for the gym.

And luckily his duties didn't involve personally chasing after any stickup artists. They were few and far between in Doncaster.

He kept the town free of petty crime. And he made sure all his young officers were well trained. At least he could be proud of those things.

It was the other part he'd come to hate.

His hand clenched around the handle of the razor as he thought about the decisions he'd made that had landed him here.

Back in North Carolina, he'd caught Sally Ann cheating on him, and he'd divorced her. But he'd known he couldn't take care of two little kids on his own, which was why he'd given up custody. He was no deadbeat. He was prepared to pay child support. But the money for the kids had cut into his income, and he'd started looking for a place that was cheaper to live.

An ad for police chief of a small town on the Eastern Shore of Maryland had seemed like the perfect solution. He'd interviewed for the job and been happy to get it. Now he wondered what the men who'd hired him had seen in him, specifically.

A man who'd be willing to look the other way in certain instances? If the price was right.

They hadn't brought that up right away. Not until he'd gotten comfortable in town. And the approach had been subtle. Don't patrol at certain locations on certain nights. At first it wasn't more than once a month. And the pay was good, considering the job was doing nothing instead of something.

But gradually the frequency had increased.

Now it was two or three times a month. And there were other duties that he hated.

Like digging in his heels and pretending he thought that girl had run away. He was almost certain that something nasty had happened to her. Probably at the hands of one of the men who paid him under the table. If he had to make a bet, he'd put his money on George Myers. There was plenty going on out at his Pine Fairways besides guys swinging clubs at little white balls. And then there were Mayor Hinton and Martin Kendley, owner and president of the bank. Both of them strutted around Doncaster like they owned the place and could do anything they wanted. But he couldn't prove anything, and he wasn't going to get himself into trouble by doing a real investigation. The town fathers had hired him. They could fire him just as easily. Or worse. If they could make a girl disappear, they could do it with a man, too.

Sometimes he had fantasies of pulling his own disappearing act. And maybe he could pull it off it eventually. He was saving a lot of the money they slipped him. You could live in Mexico pretty cheap. Maybe he could head down that way and disappear into some little town.

In the meantime, he was stuck doing what he had to.

Sage wasn't going to let Ben make the rules this morning.

"We'll get more done if we each cover some of the territory. I can go to the college and see if I can locate some of Laurel's professors. Did you get something from Teddy Granada on the other girls?"

"Yes. If dirt exists, Teddy Granada can find it. He's got a report on missing women in Doncaster. There are more than we initially thought. Seven over the past five years."

She sucked in a sharp breath. "Did they find any of them?"

"Three really were runaways—and turned up later. The other four were never found."

"Who were they?"

"The runaways were all local, which gives credence to Chief Judd's theory about Laurel."

"She didn't run away," Sage shot back.

"I'm not assuming that she did. I'm just saying he has reason to make the assumption about her."

"Or claiming that's what he thinks."

"Either way, he's got a logical argument."

"The others?"

"The others were guest workers who'd come here from Eastern Europe to work."

"Which means Laurel didn't fit the pattern. No family here would be looking for them."

"Maybe somebody who saw the argument with your

mother thought that would make good cover for her disappearance."

"Unfortunately. Do we have names for the women who never turned up?"

"Yes. The two most recent ones were Magdalina Sawicki and Andrea Dvorak."

"You can ask the police chief about them. Maybe you can get him to say the word 'kidnapping.'"

"I doubt it."

"But we'll split up?"

He waited several seconds before answering with a tight nod, and she knew he didn't like it. Too bad. She needed some time by herself. Not because he'd done anything wrong, but because she had.

She grabbed her bag and headed into the bathroom, which was still steamy from his shower. As quickly as possible, she showered, changed into jeans and a tee shirt and put on the barest minimum of makeup.

When she emerged, he was sitting at the table, scrolling through information on the laptop.

"Something else?"

"Just getting details on the stuff I told you."

"Okay."

Sage transferred a credit card, twenty dollars, her driver's license and a picture of Laurel to a fanny pack, then locked her wallet in her carry bag. "Drop me at the community college. I'll see if I can talk to someone who knows her status. Then I'll go back to the dock area and see if anyone on one of the boats saw her."

"Why is the dock area any better than Main Street?"

"I was thinking she could have gone down there—and somebody could have offered her a fun boat ride."

He shrugged, "Possible."

"Let's go."

"Mind if we stop for something to eat first?"

"Are you always eating?" she snapped, giving away her state of mind.

"Only when I'm hungry."

They drove into town and stopped at a deli where they both had coffee and bagels with cream cheese and smoked salmon which they ate without saying much besides "pass the sugar."

Afterwards, Ben dropped her at the college, which was outside the downtown area.

"I don't think it's a good idea to walk to the docks," he said.

"I'll take a cab."

"Okay."

After watching him drive off, she consulted the signboard that gave the names and locations of the buildings and decided to start with the school administration.

Inside, she identified herself and asked about the status of her sister. As she'd suspected, they wouldn't give any academic information, but they were willing to give her the names of Laurel's professors and their offices.

She found only one of them in, a distracted looking forty-something guy who taught World Literature. He wouldn't discuss specific grades, but he was willing to say that Laurel wasn't having any problems in his class. In fact, she was one of his best students.

Feeling somewhat justified in her assumptions about her sister's status in school, Sage left the college. Because it was only about a mile walk to the center of town, she didn't waste time calling a cab. She knew she was defying Ben by walking, but she couldn't help herself. Still, she kept her eyes peeled for a blue pickup truck or a large, dark sedan.

She saw neither, although she couldn't shake the feeling that she was being watched. By Ben?

Not unless he was deliberately keeping out of sight.

Her mind stayed on him as she walked along the side of the road. There was something between them. Something he was determined not to encourage. And maybe he was right. Maybe she was getting wound up with him too quickly. Like her mother did, she told herself again.

But she wasn't her mother.

She tried to understand her own motivation. Ben was right about her being vulnerable. But she was also responding to him on a deeper level. She'd been in several relationships, and each time the guy had let her down. Like Adam Weston, her first serious boyfriend. They were together for almost a year, and she'd thought they might be headed for marriage. Then he'd told her he was moving to Seattle. He'd said she could come along, but she'd made the decision that it wasn't a good idea to uproot herself for him.

Larry Brothers had been her other serious boyfriend. At least it had been serious on her part, until she'd found out that he was sleeping with other women. She'd cut him loose immediately, and since then she'd been a lot more cautious about men.

Which made it astonishing that she was eager to get involved with Ben. Especially since he seemed so closed up. Was that because of what had happened with his sister? She'd like to know, but she was sure he didn't want her to ask.

Fifteen minutes after she'd left the college, she arrived at the business district, then crossed the street and headed for the docks, a U-shaped area that had probably once been the commercial center of town. Now it was mainly a place to berth pleasure craft.

She surveyed the boats tied up, then walked down some of the piers where she saw people relaxing, taking on provisions or doing boat maintenance. She took the wallet-sized photo of her sister from her fanny pack and held it in her hand.

A middle-aged man wearing Bermuda shorts and a white polo shirt was relaxing on a nearby boat with his feet propped up on the gunwale. "Excuse me. Have you seen this woman?" she asked.

When he shook his head, she moved down the row of sportfishing boats, cabin cruisers, and sailboats.

No one had seen her sister, and she started to think that Ben was right. She wasn't going to get any answers here.

"So if someone wanted to get rid of a body around Doncaster," where would they plant it?" Ben asked at the end of a frustrating interview with Chief Judd.

The police chief looked at him with narrowed eyes. "That's a leading question."

"Like I said, at least two girls have gone missing in the last year and never turned up. Magdalina Sawicki and Andrea Dvorak."

"There are lots of swampy places around here and scores of rural square miles. I'd say you'd be looking for a needle in a haystack. And they wouldn't necessarily have to bury anyone. They could toss the body into the bay."

"I guess you're right," Ben conceded. He hadn't asked because he thought he'd get an answer. He'd been yanking the chief's chain, emphasizing that he had the names of girls who'd disappeared. His lack of subtlety was probably a bad idea, but his frustration level had led to the question.

And he'd seen something in the chief's eyes during the interview. Like maybe the guy was questioning his own motivation, although that could simply have been wishful thinking on Ben's part.

After leaving the station house, he drove downtown, found a space in one of the tourist lots and headed for the docks. When he didn't see Sage, his chest tightened. Had she changed her mind? Or was she already in some kind of trouble?

Cursing himself for letting her go off alone because he was embarrassed about the dream—and his behavior before that—he scanned the area. Finally he spotted her returning along one of the small piers that jutted into the harbor. From the way she walked with her shoulders slumped, he gathered that she hadn't picked up any information about Laurel.

He hadn't expected her to get any leads down here. The only reason he'd given in was because he'd seen that she needed some time alone after the incident last night.

He snorted. *The incident.*

At least he'd been able to stop before they both went too far. And that hadn't been easy. He'd wanted her, and they'd both known it.

She reached the main pedestrian sidewalk along the waterfront and turned right, heading for the piers at the other end of the harbor area. He was still fifty yards away when he saw a man on a bike come speeding down the walkway, hunched over the handlebars, a sun hat pulled down over his face.

People scrambled out of the way, but Sage didn't see him because he was behind her, and she was probably in the same shape as when she'd first crossed the parking lot at Decorah Security. She was thinking about her sister and not paying close enough attention to her surroundings. Like the day before with the truck in the parking lot. And now it was happening again.

As Ben stared at the bike speeding toward her like a heat-seeking missile, his anger and his fear flared.

"Watch out," he shouted as he started to run, but he was already too late. The biker came even with her, swerved in her direction and reached out his arm, knocking her off her feet and into the water.

CHAPTER EIGHT

As Sage disappeared from sight, Ben kept running toward the dock, dodging around pedestrians to get to the quayside.

He sensed a crowd gathering around him, heard people talking, but he ignored everything else as he scanned the water for Sage.

When he didn't see her, he kicked off his shoes and dived in, plunging downward.

It was almost impossible to see anything in the murky water of the harbor, but he forced himself downward, scanning the area, finding nothing but floating trash.

Panic drove him toward the bottom, but lack of oxygen finally forced him to the surface. He shot upward, his lungs bursting. When he broke the surface, he gasped in air and prepared to go down again.

"Ben."

It was Sage's voice, and he looked around frantically trying to locate her. Finally he spotted her at the side of the quay amid floating paper cups and other debris.

"Thank God," he gasped as he struck out toward her.

Movement caught his eye, and he glanced up to see that the dockside was lined with people, all peering down at them.

"What happened?" someone shouted. "Are you all okay?"

"A guy on a bike knocked her in," another onlooker answered.

Ben saw a ladder a few yards down the quay. "Over there," he gestured. Sage swam toward the metal rungs.

As she started to climb, a man reached over the side. "Give me your hand."

She did, and he helped haul her up.

Ben followed under his own power, water dripping off of him as he climbed.

"You okay?" he asked as he looked Sage up and down. She was waterlogged, but she didn't seem injured.

"Yes. Are you?"

"Yeah."

As they both stood dripping on the paved walkway, someone handed them beach towels which they used to wipe off their faces and dry their hair. Then they wrapped the towels around their shoulders.

"It looked like that guy on the bike deliberately pushed you," a man called out.

"I didn't see him," Sage answered as she scanned the crowd. Ben saw her react, but he didn't ask who she'd seen that made her tense.

"You want to call the cops?" another voice asked.

"No," Ben answered. Why bother? Chief Judd would hear about it soon enough. Or maybe shoving Sage into the harbor had been his idea.

Ben retrieved his shoes, pulling off his wet socks and jamming them into his pocket before stuffing his bare feet back into the shoes.

"Come on," he said to Sage as he led the way back to where he'd parked the car. They both shifted the towels to the seats before climbing inside. In the confines of the car, he could smell the dirty water, diesel fuel and fish.

"Sorry about your car," she muttered.

"The seats will dry."

She fumbled in her fanny pack and pulled out the picture of Laurel that she'd brought along.

"It's ruined."

"I've got another one. We can get a copy made."

"Thanks." She hitched in a breath and let it out. "I thought I'd be okay in the middle of town in broad daylight. I guess going down there on my own was a bad idea," she murmured.

"Unfortunately. The question is, are they trying to get us to stop looking for Laurel because they know what happened to her? Or are they worried about something else, and she's collateral damage?"

"What do you mean?"

"It's hard to believe that this is just about protecting the tourist trade in Doncaster. How good could it be for the tourist scene if a guy on a bike deliberately pushes a pedestrian into the harbor?"

She shook her head.

"I saw you react to some of the faces in the crowd."

"That's right. I'd forgotten until you asked."

"Who did you see?"

"Craig Fellows, the guy I told you owns the hardware store. Martin Kendley, the town banker." Her vision turned inward. "And William Hinton."

"The mayor." Ben cast a look in the rearview mirror. "I wasn't paying a lot of attention to the gawkers. How did they look?"

She thought again. "I guess Craig Fellows looked unhappy. The other two looked satisfied."

"So maybe somebody set you up, only Fellows didn't

agree with the plan. Or didn't know about it in advance."

"Maybe he did, then thought it looked bad when it actually went down."

"That's possible."

When they arrived at the motel, Ben was glad to see that the maid had already made up the room, leaving a supply of towels.

"You can take a shower first," he told her.

"I'll be quick."

She disappeared into the bathroom, and he paced back and forth across the carpet, leaving a wet trail. He would have gone outside if he'd been willing to leave Sage alone.

He was thinking that the longer they stayed in Doncaster, the more likely it was that one of them was going to get seriously hurt.

But what was the alternative? Convincing Sage to leave and carrying on by himself? He was pretty sure she was here for the duration.

She came out of the bathroom wearing clean jeans and a tee shirt, and he grabbed fresh, dry clothes before stepping inside and closing the door. After discarding his wet clothing atop hers, he showered quickly. Then he took the pile of wet clothing into the tub and added some soap, turning everything with his feet, getting all the pieces washed. His foot encountered her bra and panties, but he tried to ignore them.

"What are you doing?" she called out.

"Washing the clothes."

"How?"

"You don't want to know."

He finished, then rinsed and wrung out each of the garments before stepping out of the shower, drying himself and quickly getting dressed. Finally he draped all the clothing over the shower rod.

When he opened the door, he found Sage standing a few feet away.

The look on her face undid him.

"I should have listened to you," she said.

"Nobody wants to think they're being stalked."

"Is that what you call it?"

"For want of a better term."

He reached for her, and she came into his arms, holding tight. As he clasped her to him, he let himself release the emotions he'd put on hold while he'd gotten them back to the Beach Breeze and they'd cleaned up.

They clung together, and when she lifted her head, he lowered his. They hadn't kissed in the dream. They kissed now, their lips meeting and holding, the pressure telling him they were both skating on the edge of emotional stability.

He couldn't tell her about the dream, but he could tell her how glad he was that she was safe.

He moved his lips over hers, the kiss feeling tender and needy and sexy all at the same time.

His only focus was the woman he held in his arms. Last night he'd been trying to distance himself because he knew it was the right thing to do, even as he'd held her, kissed her. Then he'd been catapulted into a dream about her, a dream he still couldn't accept.

Today was reality. All his senses went into overdrive. He reveled in the taste of her. The smell of the soap on her just-washed skin. The texture of her lips. The pressure of her body against his. And when her arms crept up to circle his neck, he felt his heart leap. In response, he gathered her closer as he turned his head first one way and then the other to change the angle of the kiss, exploring the taste of her.

Doubts flickered in his mind. She shouldn't be in his

arms. He shouldn't be kissing her. But it was impossible to hold on to that conviction when every instinct urged him to do what they both wanted.

Sage was the only woman he had held since before his journey through hell on the *Windward*. There had been no one because he hadn't allowed himself to get close to anyone.

He convinced himself he didn't deserve sex or contentment or any of the normal things that made people happy because he'd been forced to operate outside the normal in ways that horrified him.

But as Sage nestled in his embrace, he imagined what it would be like to share more than this kiss. Not just a sexual encounter but all the emotions he'd kept bottled up for long, lonely months of penitence.

His tongue played with the seam of her lips, wordlessly asking her to open for him, and she did, so that he could explore the line of her teeth, then stroke the sensitive tissue on the inside of her lips.

He heard her make a small sound deep in her throat, telling him she liked what he was doing. When his tongue dipped further into her mouth, it sent hot, needy sensations curling through him.

His hands stroked her midriff, gliding upward to find her breasts. He felt a jolt of heat when her nipples tightened for him.

She tangled her hands in his hair, holding his mouth to hers. He loved her touch, and he knew he'd love anything else she wanted to do.

Still kissing him, she eased a little away so that she could slip her hands under his tee shirt and stroke his chest, burrowing through the springy hair, tracing the scar where the doctors had opened up his chest.

"This is where you were hurt?" she murmured against his

lips.

"Yes."

She moved her hand along the scar, then abandoned it for his nipples, circling them with her fingers, making them tighten.

Outside, the sound of a car horn made them both jump.

Jerking away from him, she looked wildly around, coming back to reality.

He moved to the window, pulling the curtains to the side the way he had the night before, wondering if he was going to see a blue pickup truck or a black sedan.

No, of course not. Those guys wouldn't honk. They'd simply burst in.

In fact, it wasn't either of the vehicles that had given them problems. Instead a woman rushed out of one of the rooms and climbed into a mid-sized Toyota, which drove away.

Ben turned back to Sage. "Sorry. We're both on edge. And we keep reaching for each other."

"Is that bad?" she asked in a thin voice.

"You don't want to get mixed up with me."

"Why not?"

He felt his features harden. "I've done things that would make your hair curl."

"Like what?"

Maybe if he spelled it out for her, it would be a dash of cold water for both of them.

"I told you my sister took a job where she had no business going. She was always into rough sex, and she saw an ad where people could sign up to be slaves for a year. The idea turned her on, so she investigated further and found out the job was on a cruise ship that a rich bastard named Bruno Del Conte owned. He had it set up like a floating S and

M pleasure palace—where the rich and kinky could do anything they wanted to the poor jerks who had signed up as slaves."

When Sage started to speak, he shook his head. "This isn't easy for me to talk about. Let me finish."

She answered with a little nod.

"I advised my sister not to take the job. I told her it could be dangerous, but she was young and reckless. For a few months I got e-mails from her, telling me how much fun she was having—getting paid for stuff she'd like to do anyway. Then the e-mails stopped. When I made some inquiries, I hit a blank wall. I was still on leave from the police department after getting shot. I resigned and applied for a job on the *Windward*, and I was accepted."

He made a face. "The first thing I had to do was lie— pretend I was interested in kinky sex. Once I got to the ship, I found out pretty quick that the atmosphere there was deadly. I learned that my sister had probably died during a sex session that got too rough. Around that time, the security chief was killed when some of the sex slaves rebelled. The owner of the ship liked my police background and promoted me to head of the security force.

"While I was chief, a couple more slaves were killed. I sneaked into the morgue and touched them. Which is how I found out what had happened to them. But I also knew that directly attacking the owner, Bruno Del Conte, was a suicide mission, because there were too many of the security forces who were completely loyal to him.

"About that time, Cole Marshall and Emma Richards, two Decorah agents, came on board. They were looking for a Baltimore woman who'd been kidnapped and brought to the *Windward*. When I found out what was going on with them, I figured we could help each other out. The four of us escaped together, and Del Conte got killed when he was trying to gun us down. Which is how I ended up working for Decorah."

He kept his gaze fixed on her, looking for signs of revulsion.

"You did what you had to," she said in a low voice.

"I let people die rather than give myself away!" he answered.

"You're not responsible for their deaths."

"I saw that some of the guests might go too far if given the chance."

"But you couldn't know for sure."

"Not for sure."

"And if you'd interfered, what would have happened?"

He heaved in a breath and let it out. "I could have been executed."

"So you used your best judgment—in order to save a lot more lives." She kept her gaze fixed on him. "The operation's shut down, right? Thanks to you."

He shrugged.

"It's like in a war," she continued. "You had to make some hard choices, but you don't have to keep punishing yourself for what happened on the ship."

"You weren't there," he clipped out.

"Right. I'm here. Feeling guilty about letting my sister down by not coming back to Doncaster. And the only way I can wipe out that guilt is to find out what happened to her."

"And if we can't?"

"I'm not giving in to that possibility. Not yet."

"You may have to face it."

She gave Ben a steady look. "Not until I give it everything I've got. Starting with confronting my mother."

"All right, but do you think she's going to tell us anything?"

"I hope so."

As they drove in silence to her mom's house, Sage slid him a sidewise glance, seeing the grim set of his jaw.

She knew he'd been trying to shock her by talking about his experiences on that ship, the *Windward*. She *was* shocked, but what he'd said had given her some important insights. He'd been deeply affected by the months he'd spent on that ship. He'd done things he considered immoral. Ironically, she knew it was because of his strong sense of morality.

The first thing Sage noticed when they arrived at Angel Baker's house was that her car was missing from the driveway, and when Sage knocked, there was no answer.

"She could be at work," Ben said.

"She could be, but I don't have a good feeling about this."

She unlocked the door and they both went in.

"Mom," Sage called.

There was no answer.

"Mom?"

As they both started moving rapidly through the house, Sage's heart was in her throat. She kept picturing herself stumbling over her mother's body, but when she got to the master bedroom, she stopped short. The closet door and some dresser drawers were open. And the suitcase that Angel kept under the bed was missing.

Sage breathed out a sigh. Now that her worst fears hadn't come to pass, she felt her anger rising. "She's gone."

"And taken some clothing," Ben said. "Unlike Laurel who had plans to come back home."

"Where do you think she went?" Sage asked.

"I don't know, but I'm guessing somebody paid her to get out of town for a while."

97

"But why?"

"If your mom's not here, she can't give us any information."

Sage worried her bottom lip. "But somebody could have killed her and made it look like she left town."

Ben looked around, then peered out the window. "Maybe the neighbors saw something."

They left the house and went next door. When nobody answered, they crossed the street to Mrs. Hartley's house.

Sage remembered that the old widow had liked to keep track of what was happening in the neighborhood.

Mrs. Hartley answered the door quickly, as though she'd been looking outside and knew they were coming. She was a short, dumpy woman in her late seventies, with thinning hair and wrinkled skin. She was wearing a shapeless housedress.

"Why, Sage, it's good to see you," she said.

"Good to see you, too." Sage cleared her throat. "Mom's not home. Did you happen to see her leave?"

"Well, she had a visitor early in the morning. Then she left about an hour later, carrying a suitcase."

"A visitor? Did you see who it was?"

"A man. But he had his cap pulled down over his face."

"It wasn't the police chief, was it?" Ben asked.

"I don't think so. He looked much more fit."

"What kind of car was he driving?" Ben asked.

"I don't know much about cars. It was big and expensive looking."

"Can you tell me anything else?"

"I'm sorry. And sorry to hear the rumors about your sister too."

"What rumors?" Sage asked.

"That she had a fight with your mom and ran away."

"We're not sure that she did."

The woman made a tsking sound. "It didn't make sense to me. Not that girl. She was too motivated to do something stupid. I hope you find out what happened to her."

"Thank you."

Mrs. Hartley closed the door, and they walked back to Ben's car. As Ben climbed behind the wheel, he said, "It sounds like Angel was paid to leave."

Sage dragged in a breath and let it out. "I guess that's right."

"I'll see if Teddy can get a lead on her."

"How?"

"If she used her credit card, the transaction will show up."

"Okay. But let me leave her a note, just in case."

Sage went back into the house and scribbled a message, asking her mother to call. That was the best she could do for the time being.

When she came back to the car, she said, "I was all charged up to talk to Mom. Now what?"

"Before that guy knocked you into the water, I was going to suggest we go to that boarding house—Mrs. Borden's— where the other girls lived."

"You think *they* can tell us anything?"

"All we can do is try. Do you know where the boarding house is?" he asked.

"Yes. Like the Crab Shack, it's been around for a long time."

They headed for a part of town where many of the older homes had been turned into various businesses.

As they drew near the boarding house, they passed a beauty supply company, a lawnmower and bike repair shop, and a business that distributed cardboard boxes.

"Not the upscale side of town," Ben said.

"The neighborhood's changed."

But Mrs. Borden's large Victorian house was still functioning as a residence, although the rooms had probably been divided up into much smaller units.

Sage gave the property an appraising look. The exterior needed painting, but the old hydrangeas, rosebushes, and crepe myrtle were well tended, and the grass was neatly mowed.

A small sign on the lawn advertised, "Borden's Rooms—Vacancy."

As they pulled up out front, she turned to Ben. "I let you do the talking with Chief Judd, but in this place maybe it would be more effective for me to appeal to Mrs. Borden."

"That's probably right," he conceded, and she was glad that he wasn't going to put up an argument.

Two young women were relaxing in molded plastic chairs on the porch. Sage saw that one of them was Sonja, their waitress from the night before.

The Czech woman looked up as they climbed the wraparound front porch and approached the front door.

"We're still trying to get some information that would help us find my sister," Sage explained.

"She didn't live here," Sonja replied.

"No, she lived in town with our mom. But there are two other girls we'd like to ask about. Magdalina Sawicki and Andrea Dvorak."

"I knew Magdalina," Sonja murmured. "She was here for a little while when I first came. She was nice. She—how do you say it— showed me the ropes."

Ben had already rung the bell, and before Sage could ask Sonja another question, Mrs. Borden came to the door. She was a short, plump lady with gray hair braided and fixed in a circle around the top of her head. She was wearing a flowered dress under a white apron.

"Mrs. Borden?"

The woman glanced from Sage to Ben and back again. "I'm sorry. I don't rent to couples, only single women. It makes things a lot easier."

"We're not looking for a room," Sage said quickly. "I'm hoping for some information that could help me find my sister, Laurel Baker. I'm Sage Arnold. And this is Ben Walker who's helping me look for her."

The woman kept her gaze on them. "Your sister wouldn't have rented a room here. The girls I get are all from foreign countries."

"I know that. But Laurel disappeared after work at the Crab Shack a couple of days ago, and I know a lot of the women who work there also live here."

Acknowledgment bloomed in Mrs. Borden's eyes. "Yes, the girls were talking about it."

"We know that two other women who did live here also disappeared. Magdalina Sawicki and Andrea Dvorak."

Mrs. Borden looked troubled. "Yes, that's right. But Andrea was like a year ago. Magdalina was here more recently, though."

Sage nodded.

"It was strange the way Magdalina just up and disappeared. She left her things here. And she left owing rent," the woman added.

"Would it be possible for us to look through her things?" Sage asked.

Mrs. Borden hesitated. "Well, I don't know."

"We'd be very grateful."

"Oh, I suppose it's all right. I put everything into a couple of boxes. They're out back." She stepped aside, and they followed her through the house. Sage glanced around as they passed. There were two sitting rooms, each with a bulky television set and comfortable but old sofas and chairs. The dining room had a long wooden table, and the kitchen looked like it had been updated in the seventies. In the sink was a colander with fresh salad greens. And a large pot was boiling on the stove, making the room fragrant with vegetables and meat.

"That smells good," Ben said, his first words since they'd encountered the innkeeper.

"Vegetable soup. It's hearty and nourishing. The girls love it. Most of them work in restaurants in town. We have an early meal so they can work the dinner shifts."

"And it looks like you've given them a comfortable place to live," Sage added. "How many women do you usually have?"

"Ten or twelve. I can squeeze in fifteen if they're willing to share a room."

They exited through the kitchen door into the backyard and across to a detached double garage. Cardboard cartons were neatly stacked on shelves along both walls. Several bikes leaned against a sidewall.

Mrs. Borden walked along with them, reading the labels.

"Here we go," she said, taking down a couple of boxes and setting them on a table at the back. "I still have work to do fixing dinner. Please put everything back neatly. Magdalina might come back for her things," she added, although her voice lacked conviction.

Ben watched the innkeeper leave the garage. When they were alone again, he and Sage each began looking through the contents of a container.

Sage glanced at Ben as he sorted through blouses and skirts.

"Are you getting any impressions from touching her stuff?" she asked.

"You mean psychic impressions?"

"Uh huh."

He shook his head. "I'm not a medium. I don't find out anything from handling people's possessions—except maybe that they should have washed their clothes."

She answered with a nervous laugh. "Sorry. I was just hoping." A few moments later, she pulled out a carved wooden box and opened it. Inside were several rings and a gold necklace. "Look at this. I'm sure she wouldn't have left this stuff here." She showed the jewelry to Ben.

"Not unless she cleared out in a hurry."

He pulled out a cardboard folder that contained a number of pictures of a dark-haired girl, most of them with several other people. As he thumbed through the contents, he said, "Here she is with what appears to be her family."

Sage felt her stomach knot as she looked at the photo of the girl standing with an older man and woman and two younger boys. "It looks like she was their oldest child."

Ben nodded.

"I guess they never found out what happened to her. That's so sad. She was far away from home, and she just vanished."

Ben wanted to say they wouldn't let that happen with Laurel, but he didn't know if he'd be speaking the truth.

Going back to the box, he found a brightly colored dress with the tags still attached. When he found two more, he held them up. "It looks like she bought some new things after she arrived."

"She never got to wear them. What happened to her?"

"That's the question."

As they were putting Magdalina's possessions back into

the boxes, the side door of the garage opened, and Sonja looked over her shoulder before stepping in.

She crossed to them.

"I said outside that Magdalina showed me the ropes. Really, we were kind of friends."

"Did she date anyone?" Sage asked.

"She dated some guys from town. Nothing serious. She did tell me once that she'd had a bad experience, but she wouldn't say any more." Sonja lowered her voice. "We don't talk about it in public, but we're all afraid, you know. We're all like your sister. She was—what do you say—a good kid."

"And my mom really did come to the restaurant and yell at her in front of everyone?"

"Yes. When your sister disappeared, we all talked about it. We wondered if it had something to do with that fight."

"Did you think of anything that might help me find her?"

"I'm sorry. We don't know anything more about it. Not really." She looked over her shoulder again. "None of us wants to get into trouble and get sent home."

"I understand. Thank you for coming out here," Sage said again.

When Sonja left, Sage looked at Ben. "Can we ask in town about guys Magdalina might have dated?"

"That's pretty much old news."

"What about guys my sister dated?"

"That could be more productive. But where would we start? The bar scene?"

"I'd say with my mom, if she hadn't skipped town." She stopped short, then started again. "With everything else that's happened, I forgot to tell you. I talked to one of Laurel's professors, and at least in his class, she wasn't having any problems in school."

They put the remaining items back in the boxes and went

back to thank Mrs. Borden.

"Did you find anything helpful?" she asked.

"Only that she left things she wouldn't have abandoned," Ben answered.

"That's what I thought," the innkeeper said.

After the brief conversation, they exited the house for Ben's car. He hesitated as he sat behind the wheel.

"You thought of something else?" Sage asked.

"I'm not sure." He started the engine and headed back the way they'd come, watching as a small Japanese car passed them. He didn't recognize the driver.

"I told you I wasn't a medium and I didn't get impressions from people's possessions, but I'm having the strong feeling that we shouldn't head right back to town."

"Where should we go?"

He turned onto a side road that paralleled the river. "I don't know. I just can't shake the feeling that we should drive down this way."

CHAPTER NINE

Ben kept driving slowly, checking out the scenery on the left and right. On the river side of the road, he spotted a long field filled with weeds and small, scraggly trees. In the center was a large, sagging wooden building.

"What do you think that is?" he asked.

"It's on the river," Sage answered. "Maybe it's an old warehouse—or a crab shucking plant. They used to do that by hand around here."

Another car passed him, capturing his attention for a moment. Not the Japanese car he'd seen earlier. And not a blue pickup or a black sedan. It sped past as though the driver were annoyed that Ben had slowed down to look at the old building.

The structure was surrounded by a high chain-link fence topped with razor wire. Parts of the weathered wooden siding were missing and also the roof, letting in shafts of sunlight that rippled as he passed. When a flash of bright color caught the edge of Ben's vision, he braked.

"What is it?" Sage asked.

"I saw something in there."

She craned her neck toward the structure as he backed up, then drove slowly past, pointing toward one of the gaps in

106

the wall. Inside was a bright splash of color that looked a lot like the dresses he'd held up in the garage.

As Sage followed where he was pointing, she sucked in a sharp breath. "Do you think . . .?" She let her voice trail off. "I mean, how could it have anything to do with Magdalina?"

"I don't know, but I want to have a look."

She tipped her head as she looked at him. "What led you here?"

He shrugged. "I can't explain it." Turning to her, he said, "Wait for me."

"You're kidding, right?"

He eyed the old building. "This place looks like it's ready to fall down. Going in there is a risk. Not to mention we'd be trespassing," he added as he pointed to signs fixed to the fence at intervals.

"If you're going in there, I will too."

They got out of the car, and he locked the doors before glancing at the rural mailbox along the road. Faded numbers said 717.

"What road is this?" he asked Sage.

"South Town Road."

"Okay. 717 South Town Road."

"Does that matter?"

"It might."

He started across the field toward the fence. The open space was not only filled with weeds but also trash and broken glass. When Sage caught her foot in a plastic bag and almost tripped, he took her arm to steady her and kept his hold on her as they continued toward the structure.

They reached the fence, which was in better shape than the building beyond.

She glanced up at the evil-looking razor wire. "This place is falling down. Why put up a fence?"

107

"Maybe so nobody gets hurt in there." He followed her gaze. "I don't think we're going to be climbing over."

"Then what?"

"Maybe there's a hole we can get through. Or maybe we can use the gate. Depending on how it's locked, we might be able to break in."

They turned right and started walking along the perimeter, keeping an eye out for an entry point, but found nothing until they'd made their way around the back to a twenty-foot-wide strip of land that bordered the river. An old wooden dock jutted out from the bank. Ben looked around and spotted cigarette butts and a crumpled pack on the ground.

"Someone's been here."

"Probably kids."

He looked down the river. "It leads to the bay?"

"Yes."

He eyed the dock, then stepped onto the boards, testing them. "This pier has been rebuilt in the past few years. I wonder who's using this place."

"For what?"

He shrugged. "I was just thinking it might not be as abandoned as it looks."

But the dock wasn't their immediate concern. "We need to get into the building." As Ben scanned the nearby section of fence, he saw a large hole in the wire mesh.

He glanced at Sage. "I'd feel better if you stayed out here."

"I wouldn't."

He could have argued, but he knew he'd only be wasting time. The shadows were lengthening, and he wanted to get in there and get out before dark.

Ducking, he wriggled through the opening, then held up

the jagged edge for Sage to follow.

On this side of the building, large doors hung on broken hinges.

"I'm going in first. You wait until I tell you it's safe."

She answered with a grudging "Okay."

He stepped through the doors, pausing for his eyes to adjust to the dim atmosphere, punctuated by shafts of daylight knifing through the holes in the ceiling. Inside the temperature felt fifteen degrees warmer.

"Okay?" Sage called.

He scuffed at the floor with his foot and found a more or less solid slab of concrete.

Without waiting for him to give the go-ahead, Sage followed him inside.

A flapping noise made them both go stock-still. Looking up, Ben saw a dozen large white birds taking flight through the holes in the ceiling. The floor was littered with bird droppings as well as boards, pieces of metal and other building materials. He could see that there had once been two more stories above the ground floor. But the structure above them was filled with gaping holes. He looked toward the area where he thought he'd seen the bright colors from the outside and spotted what appeared to be a pile of fabric. But his view was partially blocked.

"I need to go up and have a look. Of course, it may turn out to be nothing."

"But you don't think so," Sage murmured.

He made a sound of agreement.

When he looked at Sage, he could see beads of sweat forming on her brow from the heat.

"We should have brought some water," he muttered.

"We won't be long. We just need to see what that is." She pointed toward metal stairs. "We can get up that way."

"If they don't collapse under us."

He walked to the steps, testing the first riser. It was partly rusted through, and he moved to one side, trying to put his weight on what seemed like the strongest part. Sage followed him up. Neither one of them held on to the railing which would have meant risking scraping the palms of their hands.

When he reached the landing, he moved aside and grasped her arm. He stopped himself and her from stepping into a twenty-foot drop to the level below.

Switching his focus, he stared toward the bright-colored fabric. At both ends he could see something white, totally different from the swath of patterned color, and he was pretty sure he knew what that was. But he'd have to get closer to verify. Again he wanted to order Sage to stay on the stair landing, but he knew she wouldn't comply.

Above the object on this level, canvas had been draped over horizontal poles to make a kind of covering.

"That looks like a tent without sides," Sage whispered.

"Maybe to keep off the bird droppings."

"Because whatever is in there is important?"

"Yes."

He started across the ruined floor, trying to avoid places where it looked like the boards were rotten. But halfway to his goal, his foot went through a rotten section of flooring, and he almost tumbled through. Sage caught his arm, steadying him, and they both stood stock-still for several seconds until the surface under their feet stopped vibrating.

Crossing this space was beyond dangerous, and if he hadn't felt compelled to get close to what was under the tent, he would have turned back.

Instead he moved doggedly forward, testing each section of the floor before putting his full weight down.

Sage followed, placing her feet where he had walked.

When they finally reached the tent, his suspicious were confirmed. He'd been preparing himself for what he was going to see, but behind him Sage gasped.

"A skeleton," she whispered as she eyed the form laid out on a deflated air mattress.

"Yes," Ben answered as he moved closer, thinking the position of the body was like an Indian ceremonial burial. The skeleton was human, dressed in a colorful frock like the ones that had been among Magdalina's possessions. It was lying on a comforter with various objects placed on either side. A teddy bear, a heart-shaped pillow, a music box.

His gaze flicked back to the skeleton. In the overheated atmosphere of the abandoned warehouse, all of the flesh had rotted off its bones. And probably the birds had helped, a theory confirmed by the droppings scattered around. He was glad the bones were clean, because he'd rather deal with them than a body with rotted flesh.

He moved to the side, examining the remains. The skeleton appeared to be a woman with long blond hair. But on closer inspection, he could see that dark roots were showing near the scalp.

"She dyed her hair," Sage whispered.

"Or someone did it for her." He took in more details. The woman lay on her back, her lifeless eye sockets staring at nothing, and her hands were carefully folded across her middle. Her feet were bare, and he saw a ring on one of her toes. Her hair was neatly brushed and spread artfully around her shoulders. The hem of the dress was pulled down modestly over her knees, and she was lying on a platform that seemed more substantial than the rest of the second floor.

"Do you think it's Magdalina?" Sage asked.

111

"There was a hairbrush in that box of her belongings back at Mrs. Borden's. They'll be able to do DNA analysis."

He turned back to the body. "She's been carefully laid out, which usually means that the killer is remorseful."

"That didn't do her a lot of good. How did she die? Who killed her?"

"I don't know. But maybe I can get some more information."

Sage's breath caught as her gaze swung toward him. "You mean by touching her?"

"Yeah." His specialty. Nobody had ever watched him do this, and he didn't like the idea of starting now. If he'd had the option, he would have told Sage to go back to the stairway so he could have some privacy, but that was more dangerous for her. He wanted to simply turn around and walk away, but he knew this was one of the reasons Frank Decorah had sent him on this mission—to get information if they discovered one of the bodies. And to his surprise, he'd already done something he'd never accomplished before. Some inner sense of purpose had led him right to the place where this woman had been left.

His voice was gritty as he said, "Move over to the side."

Sage scrambled out of his way, but he felt her gaze fixed on him.

Ignoring his own discomfort, he knelt beside the woman. He'd done this before—with people who had died recently. He had no idea if it would work with someone so long dead. But he had to try.

He flexed his fingers before closing his eyes and reaching to lay his hands on either side of her skull.

For long moments, nothing happened, and he thought that it wasn't going to work. He was about to mutter a curse, when an unseen force seemed to reach in and grab his mind.

He gasped for breath. Far away he heard Sage call his name, but he wasn't capable of answering.

Then his awareness of his surroundings vanished. He was no longer in the warehouse. He was lying on his back in a bedroom where he'd been confined for months.

He was someone else. A woman.

She was in a little girl's room. All pink and white and frilly and totally out of place. And he—no, the woman he had become—was lying on the bed, staring up at the man who had taken her captive months ago. Her vision was blurred, and she blinked, trying to see his face, but the whole head was covered by a black hood with small holes cut for the eyes and mouth.

"Let me see you," she said, the words coming out as a wisp of breath. She felt strange. Detached, as though her mind were going numb, like her body.

She tried to remember her own name. She thought it was Magdalina, only she wasn't sure anymore. Maybe it was Wendy. That's what he had been calling her all this time.

Reality had blurred a long time ago in this sweet-looking room that was really the worst kind of prison. The man had confused and terrified her with his kindness and his anger, the two alternating with no way to predict what would happen next.

Her tormentor spoke, his voice distorted, like her vision.

"It's too late. I wanted you to be my little girl, but you don't love me. You never loved me."

"I did. I do."

"Stop lying to me."

Her lips moved, but now no sound came out. She was fading to blackness. Peace at last, after such a long ordeal.

Peace at last.

A voice drifted toward him from centuries away. Someone

113

was calling him, her voice high and urgent, but he felt no need to respond.

"Ben. Wake up, Ben."

She was speaking to him, he thought. Yet her words only brought confusion. She had called him Ben. He was Magdalina. But how was that possible? Magdalina was dead.

"Ben."

He struggled to find himself. He was Ben Walker. Or he had been Ben Walker. Before he lost himself. And now he simply wanted to drift.

A hand on his shoulder shook him. "Ben. Wake up. You've got to wake up. I think I heard someone outside."

That last part got his attention. His eyes snapped open, and he found himself staring into a woman's worried eyes as she bent over him.

"Sage?"

"Thank God," she breathed, her voice high and thin.

He moved his body, trying to get comfortable on the hard surface below him. He'd been holding on to a woman's skull, but his hands had slipped off. Maybe because he had fallen over and was lying on his side.

He blinked, struggling to focus on Sage.

"Ben, Ben. Are you all right?" He felt her hand grasp his, her fingers digging into his flesh.

He fixed his gaze on her, fighting the lassitude that had come over him. He was exhausted, and all he wanted to do was sleep. But he knew in some part of his mind that was the wrong thing to do. And the wrong place.

"Ben, are you all right?" she said again.

He licked his dry lips, making a tremendous effort to pull himself together. "I think so."

Careful not to move too fast, he pushed himself to a sitting position and looked around at the ruined building where he had been lying. He was back in the old warehouse with late afternoon sunlight filtering in through holes in the roof.

Back? No, he'd never really left this place in reality. But his mind had been linked to that of another person, in another place. The body of the woman beside him, laid out for a ceremonial burial.

"You were . . . in a trance or something." Sage gulped. "And I got scared."

"Sorry."

When he swayed, Sage gripped his arm. "Don't fall."

"I won't," he answered automatically.

He sat for a few moments longer, gathering his strength as he tried to absorb what he had learned, and wondered how he had done it. You couldn't really say he'd linked to another person's mind because her flesh had rotted away, including her brain cells. Instead he'd picked up strong memories lingering in the psychic energy around the skeleton. He wasn't sure if that was the right way to put it, but it was the only thing that made any kind of sense at the moment.

The strangest part was that his impressions were sharper than usual. Did that mean there was always some kind of interference from the recently dead? This time he had picked up a lot of information, although he wished it was more useful.

Sage was speaking, her voice urgent, and he struggled to pay attention to her question. He had the feeling she'd asked it before, and he hadn't answered.

"Was it Magdalina?"

"I'm pretty sure it was."

"How did she die?"

"I think he poisoned her. Or gave her a strong sedative in

her food, and she lost consciousness."

"Oh Lord."

"I'm not sure what happened after that. He could have smothered her."

Sage made a moaning sound and gestured toward the skeleton. "Is that how Laurel's going to end up? She won't know when she's eating her last meal."

"I don't know," he answered, still trying to solidify his impressions.

"Please. Tell me everything you remember."

"I . . . She was in a frilly bedroom."

"Like the one at Gary's house?"

"Something like that."

"Then maybe it was him!"

"That doesn't compute. Why would he have kidnapped Magdalina or anyone else besides Laurel? And why would he keep calling her Wendy?"

"He called her Wendy?"

"Right. Why would Gary do that?" Sage made a frustrated sound. "I wasn't thinking. The bedroom fits—but not the victim." She gripped his arm. "Did you see the kidnapper? Is it someone we've met? One of the big men in town?"

"I don't know. He was hiding from her. Or from himself. Maybe both. His whole head was covered by a hood. I couldn't see his face."

He saw Sage grimace. "It would be horrible if that were the only person you had contact with." She shuddered. "Like an old-fashioned executioner."

"The good news for us is that Magdalina was thinking he'd kept her for months. And she'd tried to do what he wanted. That means we've still got time to save Laurel."

"If the same guy has her. And if he follows the same

pattern. What did he want from her?" Sage swallowed hard. "Do you think it's sexual? Did he rape her?"

"I don't think so. I remember his saying that he wanted her to be his daughter."

"His daughter? Why?"

"Maybe he lost a child and was trying to replace her." Ben's mind continued to sift though the clues. There was something strange about the guy, but he couldn't put his finger on what it was. "I think he kills them when he gives up on getting what he wants. When they don't bond with him. You said Laurel is smart. She'll try to please him," he said, although even as he spoke, he was pretty sure it wasn't possible.

Sage nodded, and he saw her expression swinging between hope and despair.

He climbed to his feet and had to grab a support beam to stay upright. She was right beside him, her arms around him. He let himself lean against her, and she gripped him firmly at the waist. They held each other for long moments. She kept him close, stroking her hands over his back and shoulders, and he leaned into her warmth.

"I didn't know it would take so much out of you," she said.

He managed a small laugh. "Neither did I. What did I look like when I was . . . connecting with her memories?"

She hugged him more tightly. "Like you were *gone*. Your face was slack, and you felt cold. I was so frightened."

"How long was I like that?"

"It felt like hours. I guess it was only a few minutes."

"Sorry."

"You did what you had to. I just wasn't prepared."

He took a breath and eased away. "We'd better get out of here. Didn't you say you heard someone?"

"Voices. Then they stopped. Maybe somebody saw your car outside."

He didn't like the idea that they might have company.

She gave him a critical look. "You need to rest."

"Yeah." He glanced back at the skeleton and shuddered. "When we get back to the motel."

"Right."

Already he was focusing on the implications of their discovery. "We have to report this to Chief Judd."

"Do you think he's going to be happy about our finding the body of one of the missing girls?"

"He'll want to deny it, but he'll have to do the DNA analysis." He thought for a moment. "And I assume you know we can't talk about my communicating with her."

"Of course." Her gaze swung to the treacherous stretch between them and the stairway. "Can you make it?"

"I guess I have to."

"I'll go first. Put your hand on my shoulder."

He didn't like having her precede him across the dangerous yards of rotten flooring, but he conceded that it was the best option. She moved cautiously, making her slow way back to the stairs, and he followed. The experience with Magdalina, if that's who she was, had drained him. All he wanted to do was go back to the Beach Breeze and sleep for a couple of hours.

Moving slowly, Sage took the same course they'd crossed earlier, testing the flooring before putting her weight on it. He breathed out a sigh when they arrived back at the more solid stair platform.

He leaned on her as they descended, and he stopped at the bottom to catch his breath, embarrassed that he was taking so long to recover.

"I'll drive," she said as they started toward the double

doors.

He didn't bother to protest, but he was thinking this was the second time he'd let her do it. Maybe his extreme reaction to touching the woman's skeleton was because he'd been hit over the head recently. That was as good an explanation as any.

Glad to leave the warehouse, Ben picked up his pace as he headed for the door. It was almost evening now, and the sun was just above the treetops on the other side of the river.

When he stepped outside, he saw three uniformed men standing a few feet back from the entrance.

A hard voice spoke. "Stop right there. Hands in the air."

CHAPTER TEN

The man who had spoken was Chief Judd. With him were two patrol officers, both young and both looking pleased to be along on this expedition.

"I'm glad you're here," Ben said, addressing the chief. "We found a skeleton inside. We think it might be one of the missing girls. Magdalina Sawicki."

The Chief's expression hardened. "I said hands in the air, unless you want to get Tasered."

Ben shuddered and raised his hands. In his present condition, this was all he needed. Beside him Sage did the same.

As he faced the chief, he asked, "What are we charged with?"

"Trespassing." He read them their rights and asked if they understood.

Ben glanced at Sage who looked as white as the skeleton inside the warehouse.

"Isn't this a rather extreme reaction?" he asked.

"I'll be the judge of that. This property has a chain-link fence around it plastered with No Trespassing signs for a reason. It's dangerous in there, as I'm sure you discovered. You could have gotten injured—or killed. Then the liability would be on the owner."

As he finished the explanation, the chief peered at Ben. "What's wrong with you? You look like you went in there to get high."

Sage started to speak, then closed her mouth.

Judd looked at her. "You were going to say?"

"We climbed up to see what was on the second floor, and Ben . . . got dizzy."

He suppressed a groan, wishing that Sage had simply kept her mouth shut.

The chief made a huffing sound. "Yeah, right. And what brought you here in the first place?"

Ben answered. "There are gaps in the walls. As we were driving past, I saw something inside that made me think of the dresses that Magdalina left at Mrs. Borden's when she disappeared."

"And you know that how?"

"We went over to look through her possessions. With permission," he added.

Judd gave him an incredulous look. "You expect me to believe that you're here because you saw fabric that reminded you of that girl's dresses?"

Ben raised a shoulder. "It's the truth."

"What—do you have X-ray vision?"

"I told you, I was looking at the building, and I saw something through the gaps in the walls."

The man continued to stare at him, his expression incredulous. "This isn't the road back to town. Why were you out here in the first place?"

"We were taking the long way home, so we could talk in the car."

The chief kept his skeptical gaze fixed on Ben. "What are you hiding?"

"Nothing."

"Turn around. Hands against the wall. Legs spread."

Beside Ben, Sage gasped.

"Do what he says," he advised, hating that the bastard was technically in the right. They *had been* trespassing. He'd known it, but he'd figured that nobody else would find out about it until long after the fact—and the chief would be glad to get the information about the ceremonial burial inside. Wrong.

His mind raced as he tried to imagine what had brought Judd here in the first place. Then he remembered the cars he'd seen when they'd driven out to Mrs. Borden's and later. The chief must have had them followed, but not by one vehicle. He'd used tag teams with cell phones to keep each other informed of Ben and Sage's location. That was certainly going to a lot of trouble, but it was the only explanation that Ben could come up with.

He turned, placed his hands against the wall and spread his legs, glad that he'd left his Sig in the car. The chief did a very thorough pat down. Beside him, Sage got the same treatment, and he heard her make a small sound as masculine hands invaded her privacy.

He ached to turn and slug the guy, but the way these twitchy cops were acting, that would probably get him shot.

When the search was finished, the chief clanked handcuffs onto his wrists, then onto Sage's.

"It's going to be okay," he said to her in a low voice.

"Shut up," Judd ordered, then grabbed Ben by the arm, leading him around the building. When they reached the front, Ben saw that the previously locked gate was open. Instead of climbing under a section of fence, they walked through and across the field, where two cop cars were waiting.

Ben wanted to ask how the chief happened to have the key, but he kept his mouth shut. Probably he had said too much already, and he'd better wait until his lawyer arrived before saying anything else.

The cops put Sage into the back of one car and him into another. The last glimpse he had of her was her pale, frightened face as they drove her away.

Fear leaped inside him. What if he arrived at the station and she wasn't there? Or what if neither one of them was going to police headquarters? Judd couldn't be that stupid, could he?

On the other hand, who would know where he and Sage had disappeared? He watched out the window and was relieved to see they were heading for town.

They arrived at the police station, and he found Sage already waiting in a room behind the desk.

"I'd like my phone call," Ben said.

"After we book you."

"You're kidding."

"We're adhering to procedures," Judd snapped as he unlocked their cuffs.

Ben pressed his lips together. When in police custody, he knew that cooperation was the only reasonable option. No telling what would happen if they gave the cops any trouble, and he didn't want to provide them with any excuses for getting rough.

Sage's glance was pleading. All he could do was try to look reassuring.

But he knew how much Chief Judd was enjoying having them in his power.

After Ben and Sage surrendered their personal possessions, they were photographed and fingerprinted, and he suspected the chief was slowing down the process, since there didn't seem to be any other police business that evening. When the procedure was finally over, Ben had to stiffen his legs to stay on his feet. He'd needed a drink of water before they'd gone into the warehouse. And he'd needed to rest after his session with the skeleton. Instead he'd been subjected to a parade of police procedures.

"Phone call," he said.

The chief handed him a phone.

Ben glanced at the clock on the wall. It was now after hours at work, which had probably been the chief's intention when he'd slowed down their processing. Instead of dialing the main number, Ben dialed Frank Decorah's private line and held his breath waiting for Frank to pick up.

He'd guessed wrong. When the line kicked into voice mail, he cursed under his breath, then left a message. "This is Ben Walker. Sage Arnold and I have been arrested for trespassing on a property at 717 South Town Road in Doncaster, Maryland. It's a warehouse that's on its last legs. Can you send Mark Linton down here as soon as possible?" Mark was the lawyer on staff at Decorah.

He looked at Sage. Whom do you want to call?

She gave him a helpless look. "I don't have a lawyer. There's no one who would know what to do."

Ben handed the phone back to the chief. "Do you object to releasing me and Sage on our own recognizance?"

"Yes, you're a flight risk."

"For trespassing?"

"We're going back to the crime scene to see if you've destroyed any property."

Ben glanced at Sage, seeing the panic on her face and hating that this was happening to her. He'd endured worse. He was pretty sure this was beyond terrifying for her, which was why he kept talking.

"The hole in the fence was already there. Somebody opened it up so they could get in to leave the body. Aren't you interested in checking out a homicide?"

"Homicide." Judd snorted. "For all you know, it could be a runaway who got in there and died. Unless you were the one who killed her and came back to check on the body."

"If you do a DNA analysis, you'll find out who she is."

"What are you, a forensics expert?"

"A former Baltimore City police detective."

"And you think you know more about running my department than I do?"

Ben knew the chief was trying to provoke him. "No."

"This way," Judd said, leading them toward the back of the building. Ben had wondered if there was a cellblock in here. Now he was getting an up close and personal look.

The chief escorted them to two small, dingy cells, separated by three feet of space. Each was about eight feet square with a narrow bunk along the back wall. Next to the bunk was a toilet-sink combination. The cells managed to smell like disinfectant and look dirty at the same time. Ben watched a roach skitter across the floor and disappear under the bunk.

Judd pushed him into one cell and locked the door. Then he shoved Sage into the other. She stood with her shoulders hunched and her head down.

"One of my men will bring you some dinner later," the chief said. Pausing by the door, he added, "See you in the morning."

Sage gasped. "Are you saying we're going to spend the night in jail?"

"Afraid so," the chief said, sounding pleased with himself. "It's already after business hours, and we can't go before a judge now."

"Wait a minute," Ben said.

"Tomorrow," the chief tossed over his shoulder before stepping through the outer door and leaving.

The moment they were alone, Sage turned to Ben, panic on her face.

"It's going to be okay," he said.

"This place is awful."

"I know. But we won't be here long," he answered reassuringly.

"Overnight."

Ben turned toward her and thrust his hand through the bars. Sage did the same and their hands connected. It was an awkward way to touch, but it was the best he could do. For now. Later he would hold her tight and hope he could wipe the memory of this experience out of her mind.

"I'm sorry you're here," he said as he clasped her hand. "I didn't know the chief was having us followed."

"He was?"

"Yeah. I figured it out too late. After he showed up. He had several cars keeping track of us. One would take over from the next, so I didn't catch on right away. Sorry."

She squeezed his hand. "I'm not blaming you."

"We shouldn't have gone into that warehouse." He gave her a probing look, hoping he was warning her not to talk about his episode with the body.

She nodded.

He squeezed her hand tighter. "We might as well lie down."

She looked back toward the narrow bunk. "That bed is probably filthy."

"Better than the floor."

"Is it?"

He squeezed her hand, then let go. "I need a drink, and I

need to lie down."

She gave him a critical look. "Sorry. I know . . ." She let her voice trail off.

"They're probably hoping we'll say something they can use against us," he said.

She nodded.

He cupped his hands and drank water from the sink, then took the scratchy blanket off the thin mattress and lay down. Sage was still standing by the bars.

"Try to sleep," he advised.

"I don't think I can. Are they going to keep the lights on all night?"

"Probably."

He flopped onto the bed. "Sorry," he mumbled. "I'm done in."

"I know. I'm sorry."

He could hear Sage rustling around. Looking up, he saw her unfold the blanket, lie down on her side with her knees pulled up and cover herself. She looked so forlorn that his stomach knotted, but there was nothing he could do for her. And when he thought about it, the cell reminded him too much of the brig on the *Windward*. Where he'd sent Bruno Del Conte's slaves who were misbehaving.

Now he was the one in a cell, and he couldn't help thinking of it as poetic justice. He didn't want to dwell on that. Which meant his best option was to get some sleep. Closing his eyes, he turned toward the wall, trying to block out the light. He was so exhausted from his trip into the dead woman's memories that he dropped off almost immediately. It seemed like only moments later when one of the deputies brought in dinner. Bologna on white bread sandwiches and bottles of water.

Sage looked across at him. "How do you feel?"

"Better," he answered, meaning it.

She looked at the paper plate with her meal. "They expect us to eat this?"

"I'm going to," he said, sitting on the side of the bunk and taking a bite. "We haven't had anything since that bagel and coffee this morning."

She nodded and sat on her bunk, balancing the plate in her hand before taking a bite. She made a face but ate the sandwich, and so did he.

"What time is it?" she asked.

He shook his head. "No way to be sure."

She gave him a pleading look, and his chest tightened.

"We'll get through this," he said.

She kept her head turned toward him but directed her gaze over his right shoulder. "I've got to pee."

"Me, too. You can go first."

"There's no toilet seat."

"Yeah. Sorry."

He stood up and turned around, but he was still very aware of her in the next cell. When she had flushed, he took his turn, aware of her a few feet away, listening to *him*.

When he came back to his bunk, she said, "I think embarrassing us is part of the chief's punishment."

"I think you're right." He hated the way the man was using his power over them, but there was nothing he could do about it. And any show of anger or fear was only going to make it worse.

Getting as comfortable as possible on the bunk, he propped his hands behind his head and cast around for a subject that might take their minds off the long night.

"What was your favorite book when you were a kid?" he asked.

There was a smile in her voice as she answered, "*The*

Wizard of Oz."

"How come?"

"I guess at first because a favorite teacher gave it to me. When I read it, I liked it. Maybe I wanted to get away from my life and escape to an imaginary land. I read that first book, then a bunch of the others in the series." She laughed. "I even named my cat Princess Ozma after one of the characters."

He couldn't see her face, but her voice had taken on more color.

"What about you?" she asked.

"*Red Planet* by Robert Heinlein."

"I've heard of him, but I never read any of his books."

"More escapist literature. It's a story about a boy who was a colonist on Mars. I'll bet we both would have liked Harry Potter if it had come out when we were kids."

"I *did* like those, even though they were supposed to be for children. I read the first one, and I was hooked."

"Your turn to ask a question," he said.

"I don't even know where you grew up."

"Chicago. Not far from Wrigley Field. We used to go to the Cubs' games when we could. We'd sit way up in the cheap seats."

"But you were on the football team in high school."

"Yeah, how did you know?"

"It fits."

"I wasn't a star."

"But you were good," she said firmly, then asked, "What was your first job?"

"You mean after working at a fast-food restaurant when I was in high school? I joined the Army right after I graduated. I figured it was a good way to get away from home."

"You too?"

"Yeah. I resented my old man's discipline." He laughed.

129

"Of course, the Army's was a lot worse. I was in Special Forces, which is where I got a lot of my training." He shifted toward her, hoping to take the focus off himself. "And how did a nice girl like you end up as an accountant?"

"It sounded reliable. Not like my mom, dependent on men or working low-paying jobs. I'm detail oriented, and I figured there would always be death and taxes." Her voice hitched. "Well, I was thinking about taxes. Not death."

"Yeah."

"That thing you did with the skeleton."

"Let's not talk about it here," he said sharply.

"Oh, right. I keep forgetting they're probably listening to us. Do you think the chief will order a DNA test?"

"I hope so," he answered, thinking he wasn't going to try and push the chief until Mark Linton got them out of custody.

Now that the conversation had started, Ben and Sage kept talking to each other.

He found out her favorite fruit was raspberries, and her favorite color was blue. And she found out that he liked watermelon and black.

"Black! That's not a color," she objected.

"I can't help what I like."

"What do you do to relax?" he asked.

"My apartment has a big window with a southern exposure. I have a lot of plants."

"What kind?"

"I love orchids. I have a lot of them."

"You're not home to water them."

"They don't need much water. Besides, a neighbor will do it for me."

She went on to talk about her collection, and he smiled as he listened to the enthusiasm in her voice. The conversation was keeping her mind off the nastiness of the night. But he knew that as soon as they got out of here, she was going to try and make up for lost time. She would find her sister or die trying. And he prayed the latter wasn't going to be the case.

Laurel was sleeping when she heard the outer door open. She wished she had a watch. She had the feeling it was very late at night or early in the morning, but she had no way of knowing for sure. Her waking and sleep cycle was all screwed up.

She heard Mr. Hood banging around out there. Usually he took his time about coming in. Today he came barreling into her room only a few minutes after he'd entered the house, and his hood wasn't on quite straight. He stood in the doorway, panting as he adjusted it. She could see he was upset about something. Something she'd done? Or something in the outside world? She was afraid to ask what was bothering him.

He put her food tray on the floor and shoved it toward her, and she shoved the old one back.

Then he just stood with his hands on his hips, watching her as she ate the barbecued pork and coleslaw he'd brought. She recognized it from the Three Little Pigs fast-food place downtown.

She was hungry, but she tried not to eat quickly. He'd criticized her for that. He'd criticized her for not keeping her hair clean, which was pretty hard to do when she had to wash it in a bucket. He'd criticized her for not making the bed.

"Haven't I told you to eat neatly?" he asked.

"Yes. I'm sorry. I thought I was."

"I'm running out of patience with you."

She felt her lower lip quiver. What should she say? That she was sorry? Sometimes it seemed that he liked to hear her say it, and other times it seemed like it only made him angry.

"This is so good," she said.

"You like it?"

"Yes. Barbeque is one of my favorites."

"Why didn't you say that before?"

"I didn't think of it," she answered, hoping she wasn't going to set him off.

He continued to stare at her, and she heard him make a noise. It sounded like he was crying. He stood there for a few moments, his shoulders shaking. Then he turned and left the room.

His crying frightened her. He'd never done anything like that before. She'd never thought of him as stable, but now it looked like he was coming apart. And she couldn't believe that was good for her.

CHAPTER ELEVEN

There was no way to mark time in the jail. Finally, in the relentless sameness of the environment, one of the patrolmen came in. His name tag said he was Carpenter.

"Your lawyer's here."

Which meant it must be morning.

Feeling stiff and rumpled, Ben heaved himself off the bunk. He stroked his hand along his jaw, rubbing the beard stubble. What a way to greet his lawyer.

"Come on," he said to Sage.

"Just you," Carpenter interjected.

"Why?"

"He's your lawyer, not hers."

Sage's face had taken on a look of panic. Ben wanted to wring the cop's neck, except that he knew the guy was just following orders. Another small torture from Chief Judd.

"It will be okay," he said to Sage. How many times had he said that since they'd ended up in police custody?

Walking stiffly, he exited the cell and followed Carpenter to an interrogation room. Mark Linton, who worked on retainer for Decorah Security, was sitting at the table. He was in his late thirties, with dark hair and dark eyes. This morning he was dressed in a lightweight sport coat, dark slacks and a crisp white shirt, making Ben feel even more grungy after his night in a cell. An open briefcase sat on the table in front of him.

Linton waited until the door had closed and Ben had taken a seat before speaking. "So you got yourself into some trouble last night."

"Not last night. Yesterday late afternoon. The chief delayed our processing until he thought I wouldn't be able to contact you."

"Nice of him."

Ben looked toward the door. "It's not just me who's been here all night. Sage Arnold was arrested with me. The cops wouldn't let her come in here with us. Can I assume that this is a confidential conversation and that you'll also represent her?"

"The conversation better be confidential. And I'll certainly represent her."

Ben let out a long breath. "Thanks."

"I reviewed the file on the case you're investigating. Ms. Arnold's sister went missing, and you're down here with her trying to find the woman."

"Yes. And Police Chief Judd doesn't want her disappearance investigated as a missing-person case."

"Because?"

Ben hesitated. "Sage told me that tourism is the town's lifeblood, and the men who run the place don't want any suspicion that coming here is dangerous. But I think there might be more to it."

"Like what?"

"Something else is going on that we don't know about. But right now, our focus is the string of women who disappeared over a five-year period."

Mark whistled through his teeth.

"I think we found one of them. Magdalina Sawicki. Or we found skeletonized remains in the abandoned warehouse where we were trespassing, and we believe it's her."

"Why?"

"She was wearing clothing similar to what was in Magdalina's effects."

"I think I can work with that." Linton stood up, crossed the room and opened the door. "I'd like to continue this conversation with the chief," he called out.

Moments later, Judd came swaggering into the room.

"I would like my clients released immediately."

"Clients?"

"I am also representing Ms. Arnold."

"They were trespassing on private property."

"At 717 South Town Road?"

"Correct."

"I checked the ownership of the property. It's scheduled for sale due to failure to pay property taxes. I believe the owners were negotiating with a developer interested in putting up luxury homes, but the deal fell through when the economy turned sour."

The chief's face reddened. Apparently he hadn't expected the lawyer to check the property records.

"I spoke to the owners, and they don't want to press charges under the circumstances."

"What did you do, bribe them?"

"No. And if you want to pursue the matter, I will arrange interviews with the local media where my clients will discuss having found the skeletal remains of a woman in an abandoned warehouse."

Judd's voice lowered as he leaned toward Linton. "Are you threatening me?"

"No. I'm telling you the consequences, if you don't release

135

my clients immediately."

Judd looked as though he had chewed on ground glass.

"Have you sent a sample of DNA to the state lab?" Linton asked.

"Not yet."

"I suggest you do it."

"And now you're telling me how to run my department?"

"No. But I think it's to your advantage to determine the identity of the remains."

Judd turned to Ben. "Get out of here."

"With Ms. Arnold," Ben answered.

Once she was alone, Sage took the opportunity to use the toilet again and wash her face. There was no mirror in the cell, but she suspected she must look like she'd spent the night camping. She wanted clean underwear and a toothbrush. But she knew she wasn't getting either one of them until the lawyer sprung them. If he could spring them.

She didn't know what was happening out there, and her heart pounded as she ran various scenarios through her mind.

What if the lawyer could only free Ben?

Even if that were true, he wouldn't abandon her. Last night they'd talked for hours. She knew more about him than she had before. But not just his background. She knew the kind of man he was, and she liked him. The trouble was, he didn't like himself.

One topic he'd avoided had been the time he'd spent on that pleasure ship—the *Windward*. She knew he felt tremendous guilt for what had happened there. And she'd wanted to help him see that he'd been in an impossible situation, but she'd known that bringing it up in the jail cell would have been a big mistake.

When the door to the cellblock opened, her head jerked up. She'd hoped to see Ben. Instead it was one of the young patrol officers, looking angry.

She didn't ask him what was wrong. She only waited while he unlocked her cell.

"Come on."

She followed him to the front of the building. When she saw Ben and another man standing in the lobby, relief flooded through her. Judging by his clothes, the stranger must be the lawyer.

"We can go," Ben said.

She couldn't stop herself from sighing. "Thank God." She wanted to rush into Ben's arms, but she stayed where she was and kept her arms at her sides.

"Sage, this is Mark Linton, our lawyer," Ben said. "Mark, this is Sage Arnold."

They shook hands.

"Is Mr. Walker's car still on South Town Road?" Linton asked Chief Judd as he stepped into the lobby.

"Yes," the Chief bit out. He looked like a man who'd just retrieved an important part of his anatomy from a wringer washer.

The lawyer nodded and waited while Sage and Ben collected their belongings.

"Check your money," Linton said.

Chief Judd scowled but didn't comment.

Sage didn't really know how much cash had been in her wallet, except for Laurel's seventy-five dollars, but she dutifully counted the bills.

Then they all exited the building.

"I'll give you a lift. My car's over there." Linton gestured toward a silver Mercedes parked across from the building.

Sage got in the backseat, while Ben sat in front with Linton.

"Thanks for getting us out of there," Ben said when they'd closed the car doors.

"Part of the job." As Linton pulled away, he gave Sage a summary of what had transpired in the meeting with Ben and then with the chief.

He finished with a warning. "If the cops come at you with that level of hostility for trespassing, you might reconsider staying in the area."

"My sister's missing. I'm not going to leave until I find her—or find out what happened to her," Sage answered.

"Then watch your back." He glanced at Ben before returning his gaze to the road. "Did you find anything that made it worth spending the night in Judd's jailhouse?"

Ben cleared his throat. "You know about my special talent."

"Getting memories from the dead."

"Yeah. I can't prove it's Magdalina Sawicki. But I think it is. She was kidnapped and held by a man who kept his head hooded."

"Nice," Linton muttered.

"Of course I couldn't tell Judd any of that. I told him he should do a DNA analysis to find out who the woman was. He obviously didn't like your repeating the suggestion."

"Do you think he will?"

"It depends on how much he's under the thumb of the men who run the town."

"Let's hope he's got a shred of conscience," Linton muttered.

Everett Judd sat in his office, mulling over the way the smart lawyer had turned the tables. He'd demolished the case against Walker and Arnold in a few swift strokes. And Everett hadn't been all that upset about it, even though he hadn't let on to Walker or Linton.

The lawyer had given him an excuse he'd been looking for. He could tell the big cheeses that he'd sent in the DNA sample because Doncaster didn't want to be accused of a cover-up.

He was thinking that he'd made some progress when the phone rang.

"We should meet for lunch," the man on the other end of the line said. It was George Myers. The lord and master of Pine Fairways and a lot of other things, at least in his own mind.

Everett bit back a curse, thinking he was going to have to give a full report of everything that had happened since he'd cornered Walker and Arnold in that warehouse, and he'd better get straight what he was going to say.

"The usual place?" he asked.

"Yeah."

Which meant the private room in the Surf and Turf House.

"We have some things to discuss."

"Like what?"

"Like a meeting of the town business community."

"You mean about that girl?"

"What else?"

There was plenty else, but he knew that prodding Myers wouldn't do him any good. Nor would voicing any objections to the meeting.

Still, his mind was churning. If he could figure out some way to screw this guy without screwing himself, he'd take it.

"See you at one."

"Looking forward to it," he lied.

* * * * * * *

Sage breathed a sigh of relief as she saw Ben's car sitting where they had left it.

"Thanks again," Ben said to Linton.

"Let me give you my direct line, just in case," the lawyer said as he handed over his card, which Ben stuffed into his pocket.

Linton waited while they got into the car and Ben started the engine. When they were on the road again, he followed them to their motel, then waved as he drove away.

"After a night in jail, I expect you want to take a shower," Ben said as he put the safety chain on the door.

"Yes, but you go first," she answered.

"You're sure?"

"Go on."

He grabbed some clean clothes and stepped into the bathroom. She listened to him moving around, then heard the sound of water running.

Last night when she'd reached for him, he'd eased her away. Today, she wasn't going to let him make the rules. Before she could change her mind, she took off her clothes, and kicked them into the corner before opening the door and stepping into the bathroom.

The room was full of steam, but she could see Ben's silhouette through the shower curtain. He was washing his hair. She let him rinse it before pulling aside the curtain and stepping into the tub.

Hot water hit her, instantly turning her skin slick and sensitive.

And her whole body tightened as she took in the sight of his hard-muscled body and his formidable male equipment.

She watched him staring at her and knew he couldn't stop himself from reacting.

"What are you doing?" he asked in a hoarse voice.

"This." She reached out and pulled him close, absorbing the feel of his wet body plastered to hers.

"Don't."

"You're not going to push me away this time."

"You don't know what you're getting into."

"You're wrong."

She slicked her hands up and down his back, settling at his butt, pulling him more tightly against herself, gratified to feel his erection rising between them.

For several seconds he simply held her under the pounding water, his cheek pressed to hers.

"I'm so sorry I got you into trouble with the cops."

"You didn't get me into anything. I wanted to go into that warehouse just as much as you did. I insisted on going in with you."

She turned her head, stopping the conversation by bringing his mouth to hers. She had gone long beyond questioning herself. She knew only that she needed to be with this man, desperately needed him to finish what they'd started when she'd found him standing at the window with a gun in his hand.

She squeezed her eyes closed, trying to shut out the images from their night in jail. Even as she kissed him, the sob she had managed to hold back until now welled up and spilled out. Just one small sob for the way Judd and his patrol officers had treated her.

"Oh, Sage."

Ben's hand stroked down the length of her bare back, sending heat shooting through her. Her lips met his, entranced by the contact. Her tongue played with the seam of his lips, and he opened for her, giving her as much access as she wanted.

141

At the same time, she pressed her naked body against his so there wasn't a sliver of space between them.

When he sighed and wrapped his arms around her, she knew that he had given in to the moment.

Victory.

His hands moved to her bottom, and she realized he must have reached behind her and lathered his palms with soap because they had turned slick, running over her wet skin with a total absence of resistance that was like a lightning strike igniting a forest fire.

As his hands slid over her, wet heat pooled between her legs. He eased away from her so that he could lift and fondle her breasts, gliding over her nipples, wringing a sob of need from her.

The need built, pulsing through her in time to the wild beating of her heart.

He continued to play with her taut nipples, using a circular motion to skim their edges, alternating that with flicks of his thumbnails across the very tips, driving her wild. And then he washed and rinsed her hair, making that as sensual as anything else he'd done.

She had never thought of herself as a bold lover. But she wanted to be bold with this man. Her trembling hand found the soap dish so that she could soap her own palms, then captured his jutting cock, starting with a teasing stroke that drew a strangled breath from him. When she closed her fingers tightly around him, the breath turned into a moan. Gratified, she slid her clasped hand up and down his length with the same maddeningly slick touch that he had used to drive her beyond insanity.

Looking down, she smiled at the effect she had created. He'd been fully aroused when she'd started. Now his penis was red and stiff, radiating life and heat.

"Jesus!" he gasped. Then he continued in a strangled voice, "Don't. I want to come inside you."

She pulled her hand away because she wanted that, too. Wanted it with a desperation that bordered on madness. And his saying it made something inside her soar.

He stepped out of her reach, and she protested at the loss of contact. But he was only washing the soap off his hands and the front of his body.

She did the same, watching his hot gaze follow the water cascading downward toward her sex.

He glanced around the small tub and shower enclosure.

"I don't think either one of us is up for acrobatics."

She laughed. "Not with our sleepless night."

After turning off the water, he pulled the shower curtain aside and stepped out, bringing her with him

She kept her gaze on his face as he dried her off. Reaching for a towel, she did the same for him. He carried her to the bedroom, and they fell onto the nearest bed together. She was ready for him, so ready. She cried out as he filled her, then gazed into his eyes as he went very still above her.

"Sage."

"Right here."

It felt like she had been waiting for this all her life. She watched the intensity of his face as he began to move inside her.

She had fantasized about him. How many times in her life had fantasy lived up to reality?

Only this time. With Ben.

"I want to see you."

He clasped her tightly and rolled to his back taking her with him so that she was the one on top. And as she moved above him, his gaze feasted on her as he stroked her back, her hips, her bottom. Then one hand began to play with her breasts while his other spread the folds of her sex and found her clit, stoking her need, making it impossible for her to keep the pace slow.

The intensity of the night in jail fueled her urgency. She drove to a sharp, all-encompassing climax that radiated to every part of her body. And while the torrent of pleasure still washed over her, he followed her into ecstasy.

She collapsed against him, her head drifting to his shoulder as she stroked her fingers through his wet hair, turning her head so that she could nuzzle her lips against his cheek.

She closed her eyes, relaxing in his arms, and she thought they might drift off to sleep. But he had other ideas.

He began to touch her and kiss her again, silently telling her that making love once wasn't enough.

He was a good lover and one who cared as much for his partner's pleasure as his own. He brought her up to the high plateau again, then kept her there until climax was their only option.

By the time they were finished, she was limp and more satisfied than she'd ever been in her life. She hoped it was the same for him, but she didn't risk asking.

She fell asleep snuggled beside him and didn't wake until she felt him starting to ease out of bed.

CHAPTER TWELVE

Sage put a hand on Ben's arm, and he instantly went still. When he turned, the look of regret he gave her made her chest tighten.

"Don't leave yet," she murmured, determined not to let him put up a wall between them.

When she propped up her pillow and sat up, dragging the covers over her naked breasts, he reached for his own pillow and sat beside her.

"I get the feeling you're thinking we shouldn't have made love," she said.

"You know it's true."

"Of course not."

She wanted to pull him back into her arms and tell him he was the best thing that had happened to her in a long time, but she wasn't going to waste her breath. And maybe in one way he was right. They'd been making love when she should have been looking for her sister. Only neither one of them had been in any kind of shape to continue the search.

He watched her as all that went through her mind.

She raised her chin and gave him a direct look. "I assume you're thinking about your time on the *Windward*."

He nodded.

145

"You were there for six months. Did it take you that long to figure out what happened to your sister?"

"No."

"So why did you stick around?"

He dragged in a breath and let it out. "I stumbled on a conspiracy. Or rather a mutiny. A bunch of the sex slaves were planning a rebellion. I knew that if they got caught, a lot of them would be killed."

She wanted to reach for his hand, but she kept her arms at her sides.

"And you stuck around to help."

"Yes. But while I was sticking around bad things happened. Some of the slaves did get caught. They were tortured and killed."

"That wasn't your fault. It sounds to me like you keep ascribing the worst possible motives to yourself."

"If you'd been in my position, you would have too."

"It was a horrible situation to be in. You were putting yourself in jeopardy every minute you were there."

"I got out alive."

"Don't punish yourself any longer. You could have bailed out long before you did. I'll bet a lot more people would have died if you'd left earlier."

She watched him swallow, hoping she had nudged him toward a more favorable view of those hellish months. But she knew he'd have to come to terms with it on his own.

"There's something else," he said in a low voice.

"Which is?" she asked, wary again.

"You really want to hang out with a guy who's haunted?"

She could only stare at him. "Haunted?"

"What would you call it?"

"I thought haunted meant when a ghost comes after a person. Isn't it the other way around with you?"

He shrugged. "Maybe, if you want to get technical."

"You think of it as a liability? Doesn't your boss think of it as an asset? A power you can use?"

"A dark power."

"A power you use for good."

He snorted. "Frank Decorah likes it because he doesn't have to do it."

"I'm sorry," she murmured as she remembered what it had been like for him. Still, she couldn't stop herself from saying, "Are you trying to find every excuse you can to distance yourself from me?"

"No," he answered, but she was sure he was lying.

"Tell me what else you're thinking about," she demanded.

He kept his gaze steady as he said, "I dreamed about you."

"And?"

"We were on the *Windward* together. You were a dominatrix. You were punishing me for what I'd done there."

She tried to conceal her shock, but she knew he had picked up on it.

"What do you think about that?" he asked.

"I . . .don't know. How was I punishing you?"

"You had me naked on a wooden table in a dungeon. You were whipping me."

Again she was sure he'd said it for the shock value. "When did you have the dream?"

"Yesterday.

"Before or after . . . I found you standing by the window."

"After."

She absorbed that. "Okay."

"Okay what? You're all right with that?"

"It was a dream. You can't control your dreams."

"But what does it say about me?"

147

"That you're human—like everyone else."

Before he could think of anything else to say that he thought she didn't want to hear, she said, "It's almost dinner time, and we haven't eaten anything since that bologna sandwich in jail."

"Don't remind me." He gave a mirthless laugh. "We're lucky it wasn't dog food."

"We can have a meal at the Crab Shack and see if that couple who wanted to talk to us shows up. And we can check out Bettie Henderson again."

"You're still interested in her?"

"Maybe she knows something she hasn't told us. Maybe she called Chief Judd when we left the restaurant last time."

He climbed out of bed naked, and she had another chance to admire his lean, hard-muscled body. Rummaging in his bag, he got out clean clothes and took them into the bathroom.

While the door was closed, she pulled on a tee shirt and jeans. When he was finished in the bathroom, she ducked inside and showered and dressed. As she dried her hair, she peered at herself in the mirror.

If Ben could feel guilty, so could she. They'd come to Doncaster to find her sister, and she'd ended up making love with a man she found very desirable. Perhaps her punishment was that he seemed determined to make sure the relationship went nowhere, since he'd brought up everything from that slave ship to ghosts.

She sighed. She'd been cautious about men all her life because she didn't want to follow in her mother's footsteps. Which meant that she hadn't had many relationships. Only Adam and Larry, and neither one had turned out well. And she was beginning to think her caution and lack of trust had helped drive them away.

She didn't want that to happen with Ben. But her insight about herself didn't mean she knew how to change the dynamics between them. At his core, Ben was a good man. At the harbor, he'd jumped into the water after her—without a thought for himself. And in the jail cell, he'd done his darnedest to take the edge off the miserable experience. For the first time, he'd really opened up with her because he knew she needed to focus on something besides being at the mercy of Chief Judd. He'd been putting her and Laurel first since they'd gone to Gary Baker's house. But he thought of himself as damaged goods, and she didn't have enough experience to help him deal with it.

Great.

She came out of the bathroom to find him holding the curtains aside, looking out.

"Any bad guys?"

"No. Maybe they're giving us time to get out of town."

"Well, they're going to be surprised when we stick around," she answered, then walked to the bed and started straightening the covers. Ben moved to the other side and helped her. Was she trying to wipe out the evidence that they'd done anything more there than sleep?

They drove to the Crab Shack.

To Sage's disappointment, the older couple wasn't there.

"I hear you got into some trouble yesterday," Bettie Henderson said as she led them to a window seat.

"How do you know?" Ben asked.

"This is a small town. News gets around. One of the patrol officers is the nephew of my seafood supplier. He told me this morning. And when I stopped in to check out the clothing sale at Beach Duds, Doris Jenkins mentioned it, too."

"What kind of trouble did we get into?" Ben asked.

149

"Trespassing."

"That's it?"

"It's all I heard. Was there more to it?"

"Trespassing," he confirmed.

Sage shot him a look, and Bettie was about to say something when a man called out to her, "We'd like to be seated."

The hostess bustled away, and Sage looked at Ben. "Just trespassing," she whispered.

"I didn't say just. But I think there's a downside to saying anything else. Mark Linton threatened to tell the world what we'd found if Chief Judd didn't let us go. I don't want to be the source of any more information about Magdalina."

Sage nodded.

This time, a waitress they hadn't met before served them, and they didn't bring up either Magdalina or Laurel. In fact, they didn't talk much as they ate, though Sage noticed Bettie glanced at them every so often.

When they finished, Ben surprised Sage by asking for the dessert menu.

"We both could use some extra calories. How about splitting some apple pie and ice cream?" he asked.

"Okay," she answered, hoping that thinking of dessert was a sign that he was easing up on himself.

When it came, they took turns taking forkfuls of the classic dessert.

"I'd forgotten how good this is," Sage admitted. And how good it was to share it with Ben. Was she storing up memories for afterwards, when he walked away from her? She pushed that thought out of her mind. She should be thinking about her sister, not her relationship with Ben.

As soon as they were outside, she asked, "Did you notice Bettie looking at us?"

"Yeah."

"You think she knows something?"

"Or maybe she wants to ask questions, and she's afraid to stir up trouble for herself, given the atmosphere in town."

The sun had almost set by the time they headed across the parking lot. As they crossed the gravel, Ben noticed a car on Main Street. He was pretty sure it was the black sedan that had tried to drive them off the road.

He braced for trouble, but the car went past and continued down the street.

A few moments later, the chief's expensive truck went by. And then a string of high-end cars.

"Come on," he said.

"Where?"

"I think something's happening."

He hurried back to his Honda with Sage right behind him. As soon as they were both belted in, he took off, following the vehicles he'd spotted.

"What is it?" Sage asked.

"I don't know."

He dropped back as they drove out of town and then onto a two-lane highway that led to the road along the river that Sage had shown him after they'd first arrived in town.

The black sedan and the chief's truck had disappeared, but he could still see some of the other cars that had followed. They turned in at one of the estates, and Ben drove on past.

"Do you know who owns this place?" he asked.

"This isn't exactly my neck of the woods. Obviously someone with money."

He kept driving slowly up the road. In the rearview mirror he saw one more car enter the grounds of the estate.

It had disappeared by the time he turned around and came back.

The other side of the road was wooded, and he was able to drive into a turnoff.

Opening the glove compartment, he reached for his Sig.

Sage eyed the weapon. "What are we doing?"

"Going in prepared." He dragged in a breath and let it out. "I'd ask you to wait here, but I have the feeling it wouldn't have much effect."

"Right."

They headed back up the road toward the driveway where the cars had turned in. Ben crossed the blacktop before they reached the entrance road, then cut into the woods.

Sage followed.

They walked carefully through the woods, Ben looking for devices that might alert the inhabitants that someone was sneaking up on the house.

But they reached the building without any problems. The drive was lined with vehicles, the chief's truck and the black sedan among them.

They circled around to the side, moving cautiously, stopping when a motion detector triggered a floodlight. But after several moments, when nobody took any notice, they kept moving.

Ben heard the sound of voices. Quietly approaching a window, he raised his eyes just above the sill and saw a group of people, mostly well-dressed middle-aged men, sitting on sofas and easy chairs facing each other. Chief Judd was among them, wearing his uniform.

"A big crowd in there," he whispered to Sage when he ducked back down.

"Let me have a look."

* * * * * * *

Sage peered over the sill, recognizing almost everyone in the room. It gave her a chill to see them all gathered here. Not for a party or to play cards. They all looked grim as they talked among themselves.

"Who are they?" Ben asked in a barely audible whisper.

She answered in a similar voice. "Remember when I got pushed into the harbor and I saw Craig Fellows, the hardware store owner, Martin Kendley, the president of the bank, and the mayor, William Hinton, watching like it was a piece of performance art?"

He nodded.

"They're all here. Also George Myers, who owns Pine Fairways. Phil Davis, the realtor who sells high-end properties. And Doris Jenkins, who owns three or four of the clothing boutiques in town."

"The town movers and shakers. You mentioned them when we first arrived."

"Yes. And there are some others, too. Pat Raymond who owns a couple of restaurants. Ted Weston who owns a shop that sells local crafts and regional books. And Malcolm Varney, who has a men's clothing store."

Sage's rundown of the participants ended when Mayor Hinton raised his voice. "Thank you for coming," he said.

"That's the mayor," Sage whispered. "I'll tell you who's talking as they speak."

He squeezed her hand. "Thanks."

"Did we have a choice?" Ted Weston called out.

"You always have a choice," Hinton answered.

"I don't like the way this is going down," Phil Davis put in.

"Up until now, it was just those foreign gals," Pat Raymond said. "I mean, the same kind as work for me. They don't know the ropes here. Anything could have happened to them. Some guy could have sweet-talked them into going off with him—then sold them into white slavery."

There were murmurs of agreement.

"Until that Laurel Baker went missing. She's a local girl," Judd pointed out.

"There's no proof foul play was involved in any of it," Doris Jenkins said.

Chief Judd cleared his throat. "A body was discovered yesterday. At least, the remains of one. In the old warehouse on South Town Road. It's probably going to turn out to be Magdalina Sawicki who worked at the Crab Shack."

"She disappeared six months ago. We agreed not to screw up the tourist trade because of her. Can't you, uh, bury the case?" Pat Raymond asked. "Like we've done with those others."

"I could if Sage Arnold and Ben Walker hadn't found the remains."

"I thought we were encouraging them to leave town," George Myers said.

"That approach hasn't been successful. In fact, I'd say that challenging them is only making them more determined to find out what happened to Arnold's sister."

Conversation broke out around the room as the people assembled discussed the chief's statement.

Martin Kendley, the bank president, cut through the chatter. "I agree that we need to present the vacation environment in Doncaster in as good a light as possible, but this has gone farther than I was prepared for. I flat out don't like what we're doing. The Arnold woman got tossed into the harbor. She could have drowned. That wouldn't be so good for business, either."

"Nobody asked her to poke around town. She decided to

154

do that herself. The Baker girl's mother never even reported her missing. Either she's going to turn up, or she won't," Craig Fellows said.

"Didn't the mother leave town?" Doris Jenkins asked.

"She was encouraged to take a little vacation, with pay," the mayor answered.

That generated a bit of laughter.

"A vacation where?" Ted Weston asked.

Sage tensed as she waited for the answer.

"It's better if we don't spread that around," the mayor replied.

Sage clenched her teeth.

"I think we need to stop trying to manage things," Doris Jenkins said. "It's not working. Unless there's some factor I don't know about."

Nobody spoke up.

"Did you send a sample from the body for DNA results?" Ted Weston asked the police chief.

"Yes."

"Well, it might take a while to get them back. Like until the end of the tourist season. If you announce it then, everybody who counts will have forgotten about it by next spring," Weston suggested.

Sage kept her gaze on Chief Judd. She had the feeling he didn't like the solution, but he said nothing. Probably because these people had the power to hire and fire the police chief.

She and Ben had been so intent on the discussion that it never occurred to either of them that someone else could have been listening too. Not until a man burst into the room from the back of the house. He was wielding a gun and looked like he could breathe fire as he shouted, "Hands in the air. Make a move and I'll drill you."

CHAPTER THIRTEEN

Sage dragged in a strangled breath.

"It's Gary Baker," she whispered.

Laurel's father. Lord, had they been wrong about him all along? Had he been involved in his own daughter's kidnapping after all?

"Take out your gun," he said to the chief. "Use two fingers and drop it on the floor. Then kick it this way."

Judd's shoulders were rigid, but he complied.

Gary kicked the gun under a heavy chest at the side of the room.

"Who are you? And what do you want?" Martin Kendley, the bank president demanded.

"I'm Gary Baker. The girl you've been discussing like she's a piece of trash that got tossed out of a car window is my daughter, Laurel."

Some of the people in the room sucked in a sharp breath. Others uttered startled exclamations.

"And you're doing nothing to find her," Gary added.

"What can we do?" Mayor Hinton asked.

"Admit she's a kidnap victim. Call in the FBI instead of leaving the investigation to your puppet police chief."

"Wait a minute," Judd snarled.

"You deny it?" Gary challenged.

"There's no proof she's been kidnapped," the mayor interjected. "Her mother doesn't even think so."

"Then why did you pay her to get out of town?"

Nobody answered.

"Somebody here knows what happened to my daughter. I'm going to start shooting you, one by one, until I get some answers," Gary said. "Maybe that will break your code of silence."

Sage glanced at Ben. "We can't let him shoot people. What are we going to do?"

"We need a distraction," Ben muttered.

"You go around back, the way he did. When I see you behind him, I can—"

"No."

"You didn't even let me finish. I can throw something at a window. That will draw his attention, and you can bring him down."

Ben considered the idea, then answered with a tight nod.

He took off, moving quickly around the house, and Sage hoped he wouldn't have any problem getting in.

She turned to the grounds, looking for something to throw and found a flower bed bordered by egg-sized rocks. Picking up two, she brought them back to the window.

"Who has information about my daughter?" Gary asked.

"Nobody," the mayor answered. "Can't you see we're as confounded as you?"

"All I can see is some kind of conspiracy."

Sage peered in the window, praying that Gary didn't start shooting. She didn't like these people or what they'd done to conceal an obvious crime, but she didn't see how shooting any of them would help the situation.

She waited with her heart pounding. Ben had

disappeared, and she was afraid he'd run into some kind of trouble. Precious seconds ticked by, until finally she saw a flash of movement behind Gary. It was Ben, moving quietly down the hall.

She held her breath. The people in the room must be able to see him. What if one of them gave him away? When she'd come up with this plan, neither of them had thought of that danger.

As Ben closed in on Gary, he could see the people in the room, and they could see him, too.

Their expressions were comical. Surprise. Bewilderment. Relief. He moved faster, praying that he could get to Gary before they gave him away.

A windowpane shattered, and he knew Sage must have thrown the rock.

"What the hell?" The anguished father got off a shot at the glass, but Ben was already tackling the man, wrestling him to the floor, grappling with him for the gun.

After throwing the rock, Sage was at the wrong angle to see what was going on in the house. Fear surged through her as she rushed inside and pelted down the hall. When she entered the meeting room, the assembly had turned to chaos, with many of the people rushing the door.

Desperate to get to Ben, she fought the tide, shouting, "Let me through."

Elbows and shoulders slammed into her, but she kept pressing forward and made it to the front of the room where she saw Gary and Ben wrestling on the floor. Judd had retrieved his gun from under the chest and was holding it pointed at the struggling men.

"Don't shoot," she gasped, afraid that he was going to hit

Ben.

The chief glanced at her, his expression a mixture of relief and anger.

Gary made a strangled sound, and her gaze zinged back to the two men fighting for control of the weapon. Gary still had his finger on the trigger, and he managed to get off another shot, but it went into the wall.

Ben slammed the man's chin with his head, and Gary roared in anger, flailing with his free hand, catching Ben on the side of the face.

Ben rolled on top of the man, pinning his free arm down with a leg while he bent the gun hand back.

When Gary screamed and dropped the weapon, Ben punched him in the jaw.

As Gary finally went slack, Judd darted in and whipped out handcuffs. "Out of the way," he bellowed.

Ben climbed to his feet, and the chief rolled the unconscious man to his stomach, pressing a knee into his back as he pulled his hands behind him and cuffed them.

Sage rushed to Ben, who was breathing hard. "Are you all right?" she asked urgently.

"Yes. Are you?"

Her reply was interrupted by the chief. "You again. How did you two happen to be here?"

Ben ignored the end of the sentence. "Lucky we showed up, don't you think?"

Judd glared at him. "What are you doing here?" he repeated.

Sage started to answer, but Ben closed his hand around her arm and she swallowed her explanation.

"We saw Gary Baker in town and followed him. He led us to this meeting," Ben explained.

Judd gave him a narrow-eyed look, but there was no way

he could prove that Ben was lying about how they'd managed to make their nick-of-time appearance.

"How much did you hear?" he asked.

Ben kept his gaze steady. "Enough to know that you'd better announce those DNA results when they come back."

The chief glanced at the mayor, then back at them.

"I'll run my department as I see fit," he said, but Sage couldn't help thinking he was blustering for show.

Ben shrugged. "I'm hoping you'll do the right thing."

Gary had started to struggle against the cuffs.

"Get these things the hell off of me," he moaned.

Judd hauled him up. "Come on," he said, leading him toward the door.

Sage had been so focused on Ben and Judd that she hadn't noticed that some of the people who had fled had come quietly back to the sitting room.

"Thank you," Mayor Hinton said. "That could have gone rather badly."

Doris Jenkins nodded. "To say the least."

Sage looked around at the town leaders who were now focused on her and Ben. "Does anyone have any idea where to find my sister?" she asked.

Some people shook their heads. Others gave a negative reply.

Sage kept her gaze on them. "You're sure?"

"If we knew, we'd tell you," Doris said, but Sage thought she was only speaking for herself.

"If you come up with any information, let us know." Ben handed out some of his business cards.

After waiting for responses and getting none, they headed for the door.

Outside, more of the people who had attended the meeting stood around talking in small groups. When a patrol car pulled up, everyone's attention riveted on the two uniformed officers who got out and went into the house. They returned a few moments later, escorting Gary Baker to the vehicle.

One of the officers opened the back door and put a hand on Baker's head to guide him into the backseat. With the prisoner secured, the car pulled away.

"What's going to happen to him?" Sage asked.

"He'll be transferred to the State Police," Ben said. "I doubt that he'll get bail."

"So he's out of the picture?"

"Yes."

Judd still hadn't come out, and Sage wondered what he was still doing in there.

Her focus switched to the crowd of onlookers. With the patrol car gone, she and Ben were now the main event.

Trying to ignore the scrutiny, she reached for Ben's hand and held on tight. "I was scared when I heard that shot," she whispered.

"I'm fine."

She wanted to pull him into her arms, but not with everybody staring at them.

Ben looked back at the crowd, repeated his request for information and handed out more business cards. In answer to questions, he also repeated his explanation of how they'd gotten there.

"Maybe somebody will have a change of heart," he said as they finally walked down the drive.

"I'd like to think so." She glanced back to make sure nobody was nearby, then added, "That was a good idea to say that we'd followed Gary instead of them."

"Seemed like the better alternative. And if you stretch your imagination, it's true."

"Oh, right. He was in that last car we saw." She thought about Laurel's father bursting into the meeting. "Poor Gary. I guess he's as worried as I am."

"Only he came here half cocked—prepared to start shooting people."

"Too bad that's his style."

She stopped talking abruptly when she saw Malcolm Varney, the men's clothing store owner, coming toward them.

Ben looked at him inquiringly. "Did you remember something about Laurel Baker?"

"No." He looked around to make sure nobody was close enough to hear them. "But there was something about another girl." He lowered his voice. "I was out at Pine Fairways, and I heard two of the caddies talking about seeing something in the swampy area near the course."

"Like what?"

"Bones."

"Oh yeah?" Ben asked. "Where, exactly?"

"I didn't ask." He paused for a beat, then added, "Because it was none of my business."

"But it is now?"

"I don't like the idea of hiding a crime. Murder."

"So you don't think they were talking about an animal?"

"No."

"And you didn't report it?" Ben pressed.

The man bristled. "It was . . . hearsay. It still is. Maybe I shouldn't have said anything."

"No. You did the right thing. We appreciate the tip."

Inside, Chief Judd, Mayor Hinton and George Myers waited until the rest of the people had exited the building.

"That was unfortunate," Hinton said.

"I don't think the girl's father is going to give us any more trouble," the chief answered. "He's going to prison for that stunt."

"What about Sage Arnold and Ben Walker?" the mayor asked.

"That's another matter. They saved our bacon a little while ago, and people took note of that."

"Yeah."

The chief shifted his weight from one foot to the other. "We still have to consider the other matter." He looked at George Myers. "At lunch you said you have a shipment coming in later tonight?"

The Pine Fairways owner nodded. "I'm increasing my private security."

Judd gave the other two men a long look. "This project of yours is getting risky."

"It was always risky."

"It's getting harder to look the other way."

"That's too bad, because you're in this as deeply as we are."

Judd responded with a tight nod.

"Just keep on doing what you're doing, and everything's gonna be okay," the Pine Fairways owner answered.

Judd forced himself to say, "Right," when he really didn't think so.

Sage watched Varney stride back up the lane. "At least he told us that much. But how would we find a body over there? I mean, the way the golf course is built, it's bordered by a lot of swampy land. They had to truck in a ton of dirt to get fairways they could use."

Ben looked thoughtful. "There might be a way."

"Care to share what you're thinking?"

"I'd like to see Pine Fairways again."

He passed through town toward the golf club and turned onto the carefully tended property, driving past the large, well-landscaped houses that lined the fairways.

"It looks like they've got a rule about spending a minimum amount on your home if you want to live here," Ben said.

"George Myers has to maintain his standards," she said, unable to keep the sarcasm out of her voice.

Ben passed the clubhouse and continued on a loop road that circled the property. In back of the homes were stands of pines, oaks and other hardwoods.

"You're right. A lot of swamp to cover," he muttered.

Pulling to the shoulder, he got out of the car. Sage followed him as he walked across well-tended grass to the trees beyond. She could see large areas where the ground looked boggy.

Ben gestured. "Is that a river back there?"

"Yes."

"The same one where the warehouse was located?"

She nodded.

Out on the road one of the white jeeps that had followed them on their previous visit pulled up in back of their car. A uniformed rent-a-cop climbed out and approached them. "Can I help you?" he asked.

"We're just looking for a good place to pick up pine cones," Ben said.

"For what?"

"For my girlfriend's craft projects. She makes them into Christmas ornaments."

"I'm afraid you'll have to do that somewhere else."

"No problem."

They walked back to his car and climbed in.

"Pine cones," Sage said. "He probably thinks we're trying

to figure out a way to rob some of the expensive houses."

"Which is why I didn't give him any argument."

She looked at him. "We went to the warehouse because you had . . ." She let her voice trail off, then started again, "You had some kind of premonition that we were going to find something there."

"Yeah."

"Did you get the same feeling here?"

He hesitated before answering. "No. Maybe that was a one-time deal. But we can't ignore a tip from a local resident."

They drove in silence for a few minutes.

"It's not like you can look for a body with a metal detector or anything," Sage said. "You need a dog."

"A dog. Yeah," Ben answered. "But we don't have one."

"What do you have in mind for finding a bone in a haystack?" she asked as they drove back to the motel.

"I need to talk to one of the other Decorah agents. Cole Marshall."

She waited for him to tell her what he had in mind, but he didn't speak again.

When she stepped inside their room, he hesitated in the doorway. "I need to speak to him in private."

"Why?"

"It's better that way."

Without further explanation, he walked outside again, closing the door and leaving her wondering why he was suddenly withdrawing from her.

CHAPTER FOURTEEN

Outside, Ben punched in the Decorah Security number and asked to speak to Cole Marshall.

Moments later, the other agent came on the line.

"I'm glad I caught you."

"Aren't you on a case in Doncaster?"

"Yes. And I'm hoping you can help me with a problem down here."

Cole waited for more information.

"Sage Arnold and I are looking for her missing sister. It turns out there are other women who have gone missing—most of them Eastern Europeans who came here to work in the restaurants. Sage and I believe we found one of the bodies in an old warehouse."

"Yeah, we heard Mark Linton had to spring you from jail. I can't imagine that was any fun."

"Not much." He paused and cleared his throat. "This is a basically hostile environment, but we just did a favor for the chief of police." Briefly he explained about keeping Gary Baker from shooting any of the town's leading citizens.

"What do you need from me?" Cole asked.

"There may be another body laid out in a swampy area

near the golf course. I was hoping you could come down and help me find it."

"You mean my alter ego," Cole said.

"Yes."

Like Ben, Cole had special powers that made him particularly useful as a Decorah Security agent. But his paranormal ability was different. Cole was a werewolf, which was why he'd been sent to the *Windward*. He'd used his animal sense of smell to locate a woman who'd been kidnapped and taken there.

"When do you need me?"

"As soon as possible."

"I can leave now."

"I appreciate it."

Ben gave Cole the name of their motel and the room number, then clicked off and stepped back inside.

Sage looked at him expectantly.

His stomach clenched because he knew this wasn't going to be a very satisfactory conversation from her point of view.

"Cole Marshall will be down here in a couple of hours."

"The guy you met on the *Windward*?"

He nodded.

"What's he coming for, exactly?" she asked.

"To help me search for the body."

"Tonight?"

"Uh huh."

She tipped her head to the side, staring at him. "Wouldn't it be better to wait until morning?"

He shook his head. "More chance of being seen."

"Okay."

He cleared his throat. "Cole is excellent at tracking. "

She waited for him to say more, but he headed toward the bed. "I need to get some rest."

"You don't think Chief Judd is going to show up here tonight?"

"I think he's busy with Gary Baker."

"And what about the rest of them?"

"They weren't all on the same page. Some of them obviously still want us out of here, but if anything happens to us, there will be someone who talks." He figured that was probably true. At least he hoped so.

He pulled back the spread, kicked off his shoes and lay down, aware that Sage was watching him.

To keep from having to talk to her, he closed his eyes, pretending to sleep. He must have dozed off because some time later a knock sounded on the door. He sprang off the bed and picked up the gun he'd laid on the night table.

Sage was already halfway to the door.

"Stay back," he told her.

Looking through the peephole, he saw the man he'd been waiting for and opened the door.

The other Decorah agent stepped into the room, a small knapsack slung over one shoulder.

"Thanks for coming."

"Glad to help."

Ben turned. "Sage, this is Cole Marshall. Cole, this is Sage Arnold."

"Nice to meet you," they both said although Ben could tell that Sage's response had been automatic. He saw her eyeing Cole and tried to see the Decorah agent from her point of view. She was sizing up a man with dark hair, dark eyes, a strong chin and a look that could stop most people cold when he chose to use it. Probably it came from the underlying sense of danger the werewolf projected. People knew instinctively that it would be a mistake to mess with this guy.

"We're going out to see if we can locate that body," Ben

said.

"I'm coming with you."

Ben shook his head. "It's got to be just me and Cole."

"Why?"

"It's too dangerous for you to go," he answered, knowing it was only a partial answer.

She glared at him. "You can't cut me out of this."

Cole entered the conversation. "He's doing it at my insistence."

"Decorah Security is ganging up on me?" Sage shot back.

"I'm sorry," Cole answered. "This is how it's got to be. Unless you want Ben to drive you back to Baltimore while I look for the body."

"You're kidding! I'm not going anywhere," she answered, her outrage palpable.

Cole gave her the cold stare that Ben knew could freeze the blood in an enemy's veins. After several heartbeats, Sage looked away.

The man glanced at the black hood lying on the car seat. What was it doing in the car? He never wore the thing out in public. Only in the house where Wendy lived.

But he was out in public now. In his car, clutching the steering wheel, his grip so tight that his knuckles were white.

He'd been so sure this time. He was always sure in the beginning.

Always?

That stopped him. What did he mean by always? The question ran through his mind like a line of a song, until he pushed it away.

What mattered was that he had a girl who could stand in for Wendy. No, a girl who would be his Wendy. If she would only do things right.

He gritted his teeth. She was trying. It wasn't her fault that things weren't working out.

It was the fault of that couple—Sage Arnold and the detective she'd hired, Ben Walker. Damn them. He knew the guy was a detective because he'd done some checking around. Sage Arnold had dragged him down to Doncaster to look for her sister, Laurel.

The man in the car had felt sorry for Laurel. Her mother didn't appreciate her. Didn't love her. But he did. All he had to do was change her into Wendy, and he could give her everything she'd always wanted.

And then that nosy bitch, Sage, had shown up, asking questions, stirring up trouble when everything had been fine. He hadn't known Laurel had a sister. She must have moved away a long time ago.

Now she was back, and so different from the mother. She cared about her sister, and she wasn't going to give up until she found out what had happened to her.

What if he killed her and the detective? That would stop their investigation. But would Police Chief Judd try to solve the crime? Or would he just go on the way he had—letting the swamp cover up the evidence.

He gripped the wheel more tightly. Why in the hell had he used that damn warehouse? It had seemed like a good idea at the time. A nice dry place where Wendy could rest in peace. Now he realized it had been a terrible mistake.

Because of Sage Arnold.

He shook his head, trying to put Sage out of his mind for the time being. He had to go back to the house where he was keeping Wendy. She was probably hungry.

He stopped suddenly, almost causing the car in back to slam into him. The driver honked, and he gave the guy the finger. At the next cross street, he pulled into a driveway and turned around, heading for the motel where he knew Walker and Arnold were staying.

But he couldn't just walk in there. They'd see him as a threat. He'd have to get someone to help him. Someone he trusted with all his secrets, and he knew just who it would be.

"We'll be back as soon as we can. With a full report," Ben added. "Stay in here and lock the door." He gestured toward the gun on the bedside table. "I'm leaving the weapon with you. If anything happens, don't hesitate to defend yourself."

She shuddered. "And don't bother to call 911."

"Yeah. Sorry." What he really wanted to say was that he was sorry about leaving her at the Beach Breeze. Hell, he wanted to stay here instead of going with Cole. Failing that, he wanted to reach for Sage and pull her into his arms and tell her everything was going to work out the way she hoped. He knew that would be a lie because he understood she wanted more from him than finding her sister. She wasn't the kind of woman who made love to a man and walked away. She was picturing a future with him—which was something he couldn't give her.

Unable to deal with his feelings or with hers, for that matter, he turned and followed Cole outside.

Behind them, Sage slammed the door.

"You okay?" Cole asked.

"I don't like leaving her."

"I noticed. You want me to go alone?"

"And then what? I've got to see if I can get something from the body."

"True."

They stood for a moment in the parking lot before Cole continued. "I know she was upset, but I can't have too many people knowing about . . . my special abilities."

"Understood," Ben answered. He'd seen Cole change from man to wolf once. When Cole and Emma Richards were working undercover on the *Windward*. Back then he'd been undercover himself as the ship's head of security. And when Cole and Emma had been in the brig waiting to be tortured, he'd been watching on the video feed when the other man had morphed into an animal and taken down two shocked guards.

Cole and Emma were married now, and both of them were still working for Decorah.

Ben looked toward the vehicles. "We were out at the golf course a few hours ago, and one of their security guards was interested in us. Maybe we should take your car."

"Okay."

"Mind if I drive?" Ben asked. "That way I don't have to give you directions."

Cole handed his keys to Ben. As they got into the car, he said, "Sometimes the way I work is inconvenient."

"Yeah, but I'm not going to find that body without your nose."

On the way over to Pine Fairways, Ben filled Cole in on what had been happening over the past few days.

"Dirty cops. Dirty town administration," Cole said.

"Unfortunately."

Ben drove past the entrance and several hundred yards farther on before turning around and finding an old gravel road that led off into the woods.

"If I find a body, I'll come back and lead you to it," Cole said. "But it might be too much territory to cover in one night."

"Do your best."

"You might as well wait in the car," Cole said as he took

his wallet out of his pocket and put it in the glove compartment, then retrieved the knapsack from the floor by his feet. He took off his shoes and socks and stuffed them into the bag, then lengthened the shoulder straps. "I may end up leaving my clothes out in the woods, depending on how much trouble it will be to retrieve them. But I've got more in here."

Ben nodded as Cole climbed out of the car and headed off into the trees, disappearing into a stand of trees.

A few minutes later, a handsome gray wolf with a knapsack on its back stepped from the shadows and stood looking at him.

Ben waved his hand, and the wolf faded back into the shadows. After that there was nothing for Ben to do but sit tensely in the car, waiting and thinking.

He considered calling Sage to make sure she was all right, then canceled the idea. She was angry with him, and calling her wasn't going to do him any good right now. What would he say anyway? That he was sitting in the car while a werewolf sniffed around looking for the body?

He grimaced. He couldn't reveal Cole's secret. Well, not unless he and Sage were married or something. Then he'd be able to share it with her.

That thought shocked him. Married? Where had that idea come from? He had no plans to marry anyone. Least of all Sage Arnold.

Again, he pulled himself up short. What did he mean by *least of all Sage Arnold*?

He clenched his teeth. He'd been sure he wasn't a fit partner for any woman. Now he knew that the few days he'd spent with Sage had made a difference in his life. He wanted to be with her, but he was pretty sure that wasn't fair to her. He was still recovering from his stint on the *Windward*, and living with him wouldn't be easy. Besides, right now she was probably too angry at being left behind to entertain the idea of staying with him anyway.

From the start, he'd planned to investigate on his own. She'd made it clear that wasn't an option. She'd come down to Doncaster determined to be a full participant in finding her sister. But tonight the two Decorah agents had cut her out of this mission.

He switched his thoughts away from Sage to the night's activity. Cole had gone off into the woods alone. If he found the body of another victim and led Ben to her, then Cole would be around when Ben did his thing.

He could order Cole to leave, of course. But then he'd have the problem of what happened when he connected with the woman's memories. Last time he'd been nearly unconscious. Which wasn't exactly a great state to be in the middle of the woods at night with security guards prowling around.

Sage made an effort to bring her blood pressure back to normal as she paced back and forth across the motel room carpet.

She'd looked out the window. They'd taken Cole Marshall's car, and when they'd left, she'd had half a mind to follow them. But there had been something in the other Decorah agent's eyes. Something dark and dangerous that had prevented her from leaving the room.

Still, she kept up her pacing. What if she lay down and tried to do some relaxation exercises? Would that calm her?

She knew it wouldn't. She was too angry with Ben. He'd tried to get her to react negatively when he'd told her about his dream. She hadn't taken the bait then. Tonight was another matter. He'd done an end run around her and left her out of the search tonight. To keep her out of danger? Or for some other reason?

She hated second guessing him. And second guessing herself. That was a habit she needed to break. But right now she was too angry to stop herself from wondering if she'd made a terrible mistake by getting intimate with him so quickly.

She'd thought they cared about each other—even though neither one of them had actually declared their feelings. And then he'd left her here to stew.

She was making another trip across the carpet when a knock on the door stopped her in her tracks.

She glanced at the clock on the bedside stand. It was two in the morning. Who would be coming here at this hour? One of the people from the meeting this evening? And if so, was she in trouble? Or did someone have information about Laurel that they didn't want to give her in public? Another possibility leaped into her mind. Suppose the older couple from the Crab Shack had found out where they were staying and wanted to talk in private? Something like that might make sense.

But she wasn't going to take any chances.

Ben had left his gun on the nightstand. And she did know how to use it because she'd taken shooting lessons in a self-defense class some years ago. Picking up the weapon, she clicked off the safety and walked to the door.

"Who is it?" she called out.

"Bettie Henderson. From the Crab Shack."

She hadn't been at the meeting of the town's business leaders. Had she been talking to someone who'd attended?

Remembering Ben's warning, she said, "I can't let you in."

"I can't talk to you through the door."

175

"What do you want to talk about?"

"Please, open the door. I don't feel safe out here."

Sage wavered. It wasn't like Chief Judd or one of his men had come to the Beach Breeze.

"Okay," she called out. Crossing to the door, she unhooked the safety chain and turned the knob.

Bettie Henderson walked into the room. At the restaurant she'd been smartly dressed. Now she wore black slacks, a long-sleeved black shirt, and a nervous expression.

She looked around. "Mr. Walker isn't here?"

"He's gone out."

"That's too bad. But thank you for seeing me." She closed the door, then turned to Sage. "You remember me?"

"Yes, of course."

Bettie 's expression was guarded. "I know you're worried about your sister. I think I might know where to find her."

Hope leaped inside of Sage's breast. "Where? How do you know?"

"I heard someone talking. And I found something you'll want to see. Come on over to the bed, and let me show you."

Eagerly, Sage turned around and started across the room. She got halfway to the bed when a hand slapped itself over her face. A hand holding something cold and wet.

Sage tried to back away, but it was already too late. She slipped to the floor, her vision blurring and a scream locked in her throat.

CHAPTER FIFTEEN

Ben was sitting in the car when he heard a gunshot. Then another.

He was out of the vehicle in an instant, listening intently. What was going on? Had they shot at Cole or someone else?

He made a low sound. Someone? He had to assume that Cole was still in wolf form.

His gun was back at the motel, with Sage. Muttering a curse, he started through the woods, slipping cautiously from tree to tree, moving as fast as he could while trying not to stumble in the darkness. He was half expecting a bullet to slam into him at any moment as he headed in the direction where Cole had disappeared.. He couldn't leave his friend out there alone.

He could hear men talking excitedly, as though something had happened. Like they had seen a wolf in the underbrush?

He stopped behind a pine, trying to figure out what was going on. The voices seemed to be coming from along the river.

As quietly as possible, he slipped closer, until he could see guys moving around. Some were dressed like the security guard who had stopped him and Sage on the road. They were watching the area while men in work clothes unloaded cargo from a large cabin cruiser drawn up along the riverbank.

Cargo being taken off a boat in the middle of the night. It had to be something illegal. He wondered if Cole had stumbled onto the scene. Had one of the guards shot at him? And what did they think was going on—that a stray dog or a wolf had interrupted their work? Or that someone had sent the animal sniffing around?

He cursed their bad luck. He'd thought there might be regular patrols in the area but not that he and Cole would get here while something else was going down.

He stood very still, listening as the boat's engine cranked up and the craft pulled away from the bank. Then he heard another engine. This time a car or truck. Moments later it came toward him through the woods, and he hid behind a tree trunk, praying that the headlights didn't hit him.

He thought he was in the clear when the truck passed, but then he saw movement in the woods. He held his breath as four security guards came through the trees on foot, heading for the road. One of them passed within a few feet of him.

Hoping they wouldn't spot Cole's car, he waited in the darkness again, his frustration growing. When the area was finally clear, he headed cautiously toward the river, where he found a small dock but no sign of further activity.

Under ordinary circumstances, he'd report this nighttime activity to the local cops, but he had the feeling that Chief Judd already knew about it. Maybe this operation was how he'd paid for the fancy truck he was driving.

Unsure of what to do now, he started along the riverbank, wanting to call Cole's name but afraid to attract attention in case anyone was lingering in the area.

A whining sound made him stop in his tracks.

"Cole?"

A wolf eased out of the underbrush, limping slightly. His pack was still on his back.

Ben squatted down, seeing that the animal's left front leg was oozing blood.

"Shit."

The wolf answered with a low growl.

"Can you walk?"

The wolf nodded and took a few steps. Together they made their slow way back toward the car. At the edge of the woods, they stopped abruptly when a patrol car came gliding up the road. As soon as it was out of sight, Ben quickly crossed, with the wolf following. At the car, he squatted down again and eased the pack off the wolf's back, trying to avoid the injured leg. Cole grabbed the knapsack in his mouth and headed into the underbrush. A few minutes later he came back, wearing trousers but no shirt. Blood crusted the skin of his upper left arm.

"Christ. Sorry," Ben said.

"My fault. I saw the activity down by the river and got too close."

"I assume they're smuggling something in."

"My guess is drugs. Somebody spotted me and started shooting."

"How bad?"

"Luckily, just a flesh wound. We can take care of it when we get back to the Beach Breeze."

He got into the passenger seat, and Ben drove off.

"Wish I'd known about the smuggling," Cole muttered.

"If they wanted anyone to know, they'd be doing it in broad daylight." Ben kept alert for any car following them. "Did you find a body?"

"Yeah. About a quarter mile from that boat dock."

"And you can show me where?"

"If we can get back in there without being seen. I put them on alert."

When they got back to the motel, they exited the car, still surveying their surroundings. Sure they hadn't been followed, Ben knocked on the door.

Nobody answered.

"I guess she's still mad," he said as he inserted the key in the lock.

When he saw the room was empty, his chest constricted.

"Sage?" Ben crossed rapidly to the bathroom and threw the door open. Empty. "She's not here."

"She could have gone back to Baltimore," Cole said.

"I don't think so." He charged across the room again and checked the parking lot. "Not in my car. It's still here."

"And you don't think she would have just gone out?"

"She was mad—but not reckless."

"Is anything missing?" Cole asked.

"As a matter of fact, the gun I left with her."

Cole hurried to her suitcase and pulled out one of the shirts Sage had brought and pressed it to his nose. Then he walked outside and along the parking lot to a spot a couple of doors from the room. "She came along here. To a vehicle. ."

"I can't believe she'd just go off with someone and not leave me a note."

"Unless the cops arrested her again."

"For what?"

"For bursting into that meeting."

"Where you probably saved some lives."

"Who the hell knows what Judd would do?"

They both stepped inside again, and Cole walked around the room, taking deep breaths. He stopped short near the bed. "Wait a minute. I smell something I didn't pick up before."

"What?"

"If I had to guess, I'd say chloroform."

Ben felt his heart stop, then start up again in double time. "Chloroform. Oh Christ."

He wanted to rush out of the room, but he didn't know where to go. And he still had to take care of Cole's injury.

As quickly as he could, he washed Cole's arm. "It's a graze," he said as he applied antiseptic from the car's first-aid kit, then pressed down a sterile pad and held it in place with gauze.

While Cole put on his shirt, Ben fought the sick feeling tightening his chest. "We've got to find Sage." Even as he said it, he was wondering how they were going to do it, considering they hadn't even found Laurel.

"Sage. Wake up, Sage."

Someone was calling her name.

"Sage."

She struggled back toward consciousness. Her head hurt, her mouth was dry, she was lying on a hard surface with her hands cuffed behind her back, and she was sure she didn't want to be wherever she was.

But the urgency of the voice penetrated the fog in her brain, and when she realized who was speaking, her eyes blinked open.

"Laurel."

"Thank God. I've been so worried when you wouldn't wake up."

Sage awkwardly pushed herself to a sitting position and squinted at her sister. It was easier to see with one eye closed.

What she saw made her gasp. Laurel's hair had been

dyed blond, she was dressed in little girl pajamas, and her skin was pale. "Are you okay? What happened to you?"

"I woke up here and found out he'd dyed my hair."

Sage looked around the frilly room. "Who is he?"

"I wish I knew. He's weird. One minute he's trying to be nice. Then he gets so angry." She paused and stared at her sister. "And now he's brought you here, and I don't know why. Did he go to Baltimore to get you?"

"No. I've been in Doncaster with a private detective for a few days looking for you." She tried to move toward her sister and found she was restrained by a chain attached to the cuffs that tied her hands.

"Then I guess I got you captured," Laurel said.

"It's not your fault. I was desperate to find you." She looked around the room and fought to control her panic. "How long have I been here?"

"I'm not sure. There's no clock. I never even know if it's night or day. But I think he comes in late at night. And sometimes in the morning."

"When Ben comes back to the motel, he'll see I'm missing," she said.

"Who's Ben?"

"An agent from Decorah Security. I hired them to help me find you." It was what she didn't say that hung between them in the charged air. She and Ben had struck out, and now the guy who had Laurel also had Sage.

Laurel moved toward the end of the bed and stretched out her arm, but she couldn't reach her sister. "I saw him bring you in here," she said in a voice she couldn't hold steady.

"You keep saying 'him.' It was Bettie Henderson who came to my motel room and said she had information about you. She—" The memory seemed just out of focus, and she struggled through the haze. "She put something over my mouth."

"Bettie Henderson!" Laurel gasped. "Yes, I remember talking to her outside the restaurant after my shift. And then—" She stopped and started again. "I didn't realize this had anything to do with her."

"She must be working with the guy."

Laurel nodded, obviously trying to wrap her head around the new information.

Sage kept her gaze on her sister. "He hasn't done anything to you? I mean . . . hurt you. . . raped you?"

"No. He wants me to be his little girl—and to like him, only he can't hold it together."

"What else can you tell me about him?"

"Nothing that's going to help. I've wracked my brain, trying to figure him out. He always wears a hood over his head, and it muffles his voice." She stopped and gave a mirthless laugh. "I call him Mr. Hood. But not to his face. Even if he's someone I know, I wouldn't be able to figure it out."

She stopped and took a breath. "He acts like I'm a little kid. He wants to watch me play. And if I don't do it right, he blows up, and then he cries and stamps out."

"He cries?"

"Yes. And he calls me Wendy. I guess he wants me to be someone with that name."

Wendy. The name triggered a memory, and she gasped.

"What?"

"Ben and I found a body," she said slowly. She remembered how he'd touched the bones in the abandoned warehouse. Ben had gotten into the woman's final memories. She'd been killed by a man who wore a black hood and called her Wendy. Chill bumps rose up on her arms.

"What?" Laurel said again as she zeroed in on Sage's expression.

She didn't want to tell her sister about the hood and the name.

"Nothing," she murmured.

"It's got to be something."

Sage switched tactics. "This guy must be an emotional mess, but somehow he's gotten Bettie Henderson to work with him," she said. "Did he tell you *his* name?"

"He wanted me to call him Dad. But once he said his name was Jim."

"You believe him?"

"I don't know what to believe."

"Suppose he and Bettie are married?" Sage theorized. "That might explain why she's helping him. Like that horrible guy in California who kept that girl captive for eighteen years or something. His wife helped him."

"That could be right," Laurel replied. "But I can't imagine anyone living with him."

"Maybe they had a child and lost her, and he's trying to recreate their life together."

"But Bettie never comes here with him."

Sage nodded. Some screwed-up guy had taken Laurel captive, apparently to play like she was his little girl. He'd kidnapped other women and killed them. And now she was here, too.

She didn't want to think about what that meant. Instead she wanted to think about Ben. About him discovering her missing—then trying to find her.

At that first meeting, she hadn't liked him. But she'd gradually realized he was rock solid and steady. If anyone could figure out where she was now, he could. But did he even have a clue where to look? Maybe he'd found that other body tonight. Maybe he'd gotten something he could use from her. She had to hope that was true.

"Now you're here, and I don't know what to think," Laurel said, echoing her earlier thoughts.

"Did Bettie bring me in here?"

"No. It was him."

What did it all mean? Sage wondered. Nothing good, she was sure.

"If someone took her, do you have any idea who it could be?" Cole asked Ben.

He shook his head. "If I knew that, we would already have found her sister."

"I guess you know it's not the father because he's in jail. Do you think it has anything to do with the smuggling?"

Ben shook his head. "Not directly. But the people involved are probably worried that our poking around looking for Laurel could stir up trouble for them."

"And who do you think the smugglers are?"

"Certainly the guy who owns the golf course, George Myers. Either that or they're doing it right under his nose." He thought for a moment. "And the chief of police, Everett Judd, has to be looking the other way. In fact, maybe that's why he got so hyper when he found us at that old warehouse. Maybe it's an alternate drop-off point for the goods they're bringing in. That would make sense. If they vary the location, there's less chance of getting caught in either place."

Ben dragged in a breath and let it out. "I want to lay my hands on that body. But I think going out there without police protection is a mistake, especially tonight." He thought for a moment. "Our best move is to tell Judd we've got proof that he's involved in the smuggling. Let's see if we can force him to go out there with us and protect us from the other guys."

"You know where to find him?"

"We took a tour of town when we first got here, and Sage showed me his house." As he said her name, his insides clenched. He'd been trying to avoid thinking about what might have happened to her, but it was impossible not to let his imagination run wild.

He ruthlessly cut off the images running through his mind.

"Let's go lean on Chief Judd," Cole said.

"You're sure you're okay?"

"I told you, it's minor."

They drove past the chief's house and parked up the road, then made their way cautiously back through the woods.

"What are we going to do when we get there?" Cole asked.

"Make sure he's alone, then knock on the door. If we tried to break in, he'd have the perfect excuse to shoot us."

"Where do you want me when you're getting his attention?"

"Out of sight at the side of the porch."

"With my gun?"

"Yes."

"If this goes south, we could be in big trouble. Look what happened when he caught you trespassing."

"Sage is already in big trouble," Ben clipped out, then ordered himself to calm down. "Sorry. I realize you don't have to be involved in this."

"I'm not leaving you twisting in the wind. You're the reason Emma and I got off the *Windward*."

"I think it was a joint effort. And let's not waste our breath arguing about it."

Cole nodded tightly, then asked, "You think the chief is

withholding information about the kidnapper?"

"I don't know."

When they reached the property, Ben motioned for his friend to stay in the woods while he crossed the lawn to the house. Through the window he spotted the chief in the living room, drinking beer and watching a recorded baseball game on a big-screen TV. Several more cans sat on the table in front of him.

Ben beckoned to Cole, who joined him on the porch and took up the position they had discussed.

Ben's heart was pounding hard as he rang the bell and waited while the light clicked on and the chief eyed him through the panes of glass in the top of the door.

"What are you doing here?" he called out, his voice both surprised and belligerent.

"Sage Arnold has been kidnapped. I need your help."

"No shit?"

When Judd opened the door, Ben pushed him inside without waiting for an invitation.

The chief went for his weapon, but Ben grabbed his gun arm and pushed him farther into the hall. Cole followed.

"What the fuck is going on?" Judd bellowed, looking from one invader to the other. "Were you shitting me about Arnold?"

"No," Ben answered.

While he held his gun on Judd, Cole disarmed the chief and checked to make sure he didn't have another gun in an ankle holster.

"Who the fuck are you?" the lawman demanded.

"Cole Marshall from Decorah Security."

"What do you want? Whatever it is, you and your buddy are in a heap of trouble."

"Let's sit down." Ben gestured toward the living room.

"Like I said, we're here to ask for your help."

Judd resumed his place on the sofa. Ben and Cole took chairs on either side of him.

The chief fixed Ben with a combative glare. "You have a damn funny way of asking."

"True, but we're going to give you a little incentive." He kept his gaze fixed on Judd, gauging the man's reaction. "We know there's a smuggling operation going on out at Pine Fairways—with a delivery having arrived tonight. And we know the alternate location is the warehouse where we found that body. Well, not in the building, but outside at the dock. That's why you were so hot under the collar when you found me and Sage poking around there."

Ben had expected the chief to react with anger or outraged denial. In fact, to Ben's astonishment, the man's expression changed to one of relief. "You know all that?"

"Yes."

"So the operation's blown, whatever happens now?"

"Yeah."

Judd looked thoughtful. "But the way it works, the guy who testifies against the others can cut a deal."

Ben nodded.

"So if I'm willing to spill my guts to the State's Attorney, you think that smart lawyer who came down here and got you out of the pokey could get me a good deal?"

Ben struggled to keep his jaw from dropping open.

"Yeah, I see you're surprised," the chief continued. "But I've been thinking for a couple of years now that I was in deep shit, and I didn't know how to dig my way out. Did you ever get yourself into something that you wished to hell you could get out of—only you knew you were stuck?"

Ben glanced at Cole, then back at the chief. "As a matter of fact, yes." The chief's words had zinged him back to the six months of horror he'd spent on the *Windward*—until Cole and Emma Richards had shown up.

"And now you can help me get out of this *town* from hell. On the surface it looks peaceful." He laughed mirthlessly. "Poke in the swamp a little bit, and dead bodies come floating to the surface."

"I think you can get a good deal, if you're willing to testify against the others. Who else is involved besides George Myers?"

"The mayor."

"What are you bringing in?"

Judd kept his gaze steady. "I'm not bringing anything. Myers and Hinton make all the arrangement. And it's Myers in charge, not the mayor. I get the feeling Myers has something on him, but I don't know what."

"And we stumbled into the middle of it tonight," Ben muttered.

"What does it mean that you're here?" Laurel repeated her earlier question, her voice not quite steady.

"That he knew I was looking for you, and he wanted to stop me." Sage focused on her sister. "I'm not giving up. You can't either." She scrunched herself into a ball, then carefully worked her body through the loop formed by her arms and the handcuffs. After some effort she was able to slip her hands from her back to her front.

Cautiously, she stood up and walked on shaky legs as far as the chain would allow.

"You come this way," she said to Laurel.

Her sister got off of the bed and came toward her. If they reached out their hands, they could touch each other, but that was all.

Sage turned around and looked at the place where her

chain was attached to the wall, then to the place where
Laurel's chain was attached. The wall mounts were different.
Laurel's was fixed to a metal plate. Hers was on a bolt that
went directly into the wall. "What have you got over there?"
she asked Laurel. "A knife? A fork? Anything sharp?"

"I have a fork."

"Give it here."

Again they walked toward each other. Laurel reached out
and handed her the stainless steel utensil. She brought it
back to the place where the bolt was secured to the wall and
stabbed at the plaster, having to move both hands at once
because of the cuffs. A tiny bit of plaster came off.

Laurel watched her. "That's going to take all day,
especially with your hands like that."

"You have a better idea?"

"No."

Sage went back to working on the wall, and as she dug at
the plaster and twisted with the fork tines, she thought about
Ben. About their relationship. He was the kind of man she'd
wanted since she was a teenager. She'd finally found him,
and she might not be alive to have anything more with him.
Not if the man in the hood came back before she dug the
chain out of the wall.

CHAPTER SIXTEEN

Judd answered Ben's question about the smuggling operation. "I get a cut for making sure nobody interferes with the operation. They're bringing in anything they can make money on. Mary Jane. Coke. Fake prescription drugs. From here it gets trucked to Baltimore."

Ben made an angry sound.

"People who need the real drugs and take that stuff can die," Cole said.

"I fought against that, but I don't have the power in this game. Once I let them suck me in, that was it."

"And you sent a man to follow Sage and try to run her down," Ben accused.

The chief kept his gaze steady. "I sent a man to sniff out what she was doin'. It wasn't my idea to try and run her down."

"Or run us off the road after dinner that first night?"

"Sorry about that. George Myers wanted to discourage you."

Ben kept his gaze on the chief. Although Ben wanted to despise the guy, he understood the man better than he was going to admit. But neither of their past sins was important now.

"I want your word you'll help me find Sage and Laurel."

"You're sure Sage is kidnapped?"

"Ninety nine percent. I mean, what else could it be?"

"She could have decided to go back to Baltimore."

"She was adamant that she was going to find her sister. She wouldn't just give up. And even if she had, she didn't take the car. How would she have gotten out of here? And she couldn't have called her mom to give her a ride because someone paid off Angel Baker to butt out."

Judd sighed. "Yeah."

"And we smelled chloroform in the motel room," Cole added.

"Jesus. I guess you're right, then."

Ben kept his voice even. "I have to think the kidnapper went after her because we were trying to find Laurel—unlike anybody else in town. He was safe until we got here."

The chief gave a little nod.

"You ever get a report of two women missing within days of each other?"

"No."

"Which means that both of them are in extreme danger," Ben said. "Because the kidnapper is acting out of pattern. We have to assume he took Sage because of the investigation, and now he's going to get rid of them both."

He kept his gaze fixed on the chief. "Laurel might have been more aware that something could happen to her if you'd acknowledged the other kidnappings."

"I understand that," Judd clipped out. "And as far as I'm concerned, the cover-up ends now."

"Then let's find Sage and Laurel and stop this guy from killing again." He nodded at Cole. "We went out to have a look around the area bordering the Pine Fairways tonight—and unfortunately we left Sage at the motel." He grimaced.

"Because I thought the golf course was dangerous."

"You were staking out the smuggling operation?" Judd asked.

"No. We stumbled into that." Ben continued to watch the chief.

"Do you have any idea who's got the women?"

"I've been over it in my mind a million times, and my best guess would be George Myers. He's got plenty of space to hide somebody and plenty of money to set up anything he wants. Then there's William Hinton. He's got it into his head that he can do anything he wants around here."

"And if Hinton or Myers had kidnapped Sage and Laurel, you wouldn't be protecting them now?"

Judd blustered at that. "No."

"But you kept the kidnappings quiet for years."

"It was just foreign girls."

"They don't count?"

"I guess the town fathers don't think so. Not if it means screwing up the tourist trade."

"What about Laurel?"

"They told me to treat her disappearance the same way."

Ben made a snorting sound. "That's just wonderful."

"Like I said, I couldn't refuse."

"They have something else on you?"

"Only what I mentioned. Once I agreed to let them bring illegal stuff in, I was as much a part of the operation as they were."

"Is there anything you think would help find Sage and Laurel? Anything at all?"

Judd shook his head. "I wish there were."

Ben clenched his hands into fists. "If you don't have any leads, we're going back out to Pine Fairways. And you're going to make sure nobody stops us."

193

"What's the golf course got to do with anything?"

Cole answered. "Ben got a tip that there was another body out there. We went out to investigate, and I found it."

"Wait a minute. That was *you* out there tonight?"

"Yes."

"The way I heard it, they shot at a big dog."

Cole shrugged. "I guess they had it wrong. Or they didn't want to admit they shot at a person."

Judd flapped his hands in frustration. "Christ!"

"The three of us are going out there again," Ben said. "And this time you'll make sure nobody interferes."

"And what are you going to do?"

"Examine the body for clues," Ben answered. "Like I did at the warehouse." He didn't explain the unusual way he did that.

"And you really think that will lead us to the guy who snatched Laurel and Sage?"

"It's our best shot," Ben answered. "Unless you can come up with something better."

Judd shook his head; then he rose. "I'll get some shovels."

"No need," Cole answered. "The body was lying on a blanket, on top of the ground."

The chief looked at Ben. "Sounds like the way that other girl was laid out at the warehouse."

"Exactly."

And Laurel was next. Laurel and Sage, he thought with a grimace. Unless he could find them first.

He wanted to scream in anguish and rage. He wanted to sock the chief in the jaw for all the times he'd looked the other way, but he kept himself under control. An emotional outburst wasn't going to do them any good. He had to keep cool—and do what he had to do.

194

They went in two vehicles, with Ben in the lead and the chief following in his fancy truck.

"You trust him?" Cole asked. "I mean, you think that when we get there, we won't find a bunch of guys with guns pointed at us?"

"I think he's telling the truth. He hates the position they pushed him into, and he wants to get out. And I do think he wants to find Laurel and Sage—and figure out who killed the other women. That will count in his favor, too."

"But when push comes to shove, will he cave?"

"I have to take a chance on him. I know what he's going through. That feeling of being trapped. And I understand why he wants to get himself out from under the thumb of Myers and Hinton." Ben swallowed hard. "But I'm sorry I dragged you into this."

"You didn't drag me." Cole paused before saying, "We need to focus on business. I didn't have a chance to mark the location. I'll have to find it again."

"But you think you can?"

"I caught the scent before. It will lead me back." He laughed. "Even when I'm not in wolf form, I've got a pretty effective nose."

"I noticed."

This time, they drove onto the golf course property, and Cole directed Ben to the closest place to park.

Judd eased up behind them.

As they all stood on the shoulder, one of the private security cars pulled up, and a uniformed guard got out. Ben tensed as he anticipated a confrontation.

The guard looked questioningly at Judd. "Sir?"

"Police business," the chief snapped.

"Was this cleared with Mr. Myers?"

"I said, police business."

Ben was astonished when the guard pressed the issue. "What is the nature of the business?"

"A murder investigation," Judd answered, punching out the words. "I suggest you leave us to it."

The guard looked like he wanted to say something else. Instead he got back in his vehicle and drove away.

"Thanks," Ben said.

"You see how it is."

"I do."

Ben looked up at the sky, and he could see dawn approaching. "We'd better get moving. I think we're safest if you come with us."

Judd brought up the rear as they headed into the woods. The ground was boggy, and sometimes they had to walk around patches of standing water.

"Should have worn boots," Judd muttered. He looked at Cole. "I guess you already ruined one pair of shoes."

"Yeah," the Decorah agent answered without bothering to explain that he hadn't been wearing shoes on his last trip to the area.

He walked rapidly, dragging in drafts of air as he went, and Ben knew he was sniffing out the remains.

He finally stopped in a stand of pines and pointed. "Over there."

"You stay here," Ben said to the other two men.

"You don't want my help?" Judd asked.

"Not now." He turned to Cole. "If I'm not back in ten minutes, come get me."

When Cole nodded, he walked toward the pines. The last thing he wanted to do was touch another body. It had taken a hell of a lot out of him last time, but he was going to do it again, because Sage was missing, and he had to find her.

After a few minutes, he found a place where a blanket

had been spread on the ground. It was partially covered with pine needles, as were the skeletal remains. It appeared to be a young woman with her hands folded across her middle and her hair dyed a vivid blond, like the previous victim.

Ben knelt down and examined her. Unlike the remains they'd found in the warehouse, this one was dressed in a torn and faded waitress uniform. Was it what she'd been wearing when she was kidnapped?

The outfit gave him pause. A waitress. Like Laurel. And as best he could remember, the same uniform as the servers wore at the Crab Shack. Where Laurel worked.

He studied the remains, trying to figure out as much as he could.

Like the victim in the warehouse, this one was carefully arranged. He knelt beside her, flexing his fingers. After the last time, he dreaded touching the damn thing.

But if it would help him find Sage, he would do it.

Closing his eyes, he pressed his hands to the skull.

Immediately, his vision swam, and a sick feeling rose in his throat. As before, his own consciousness faded away. He was no longer Ben Walker. Instead he was another person. A frightened woman who know she was going to die.

Her lips moved. Although no sound came out, in her mind she was pleading for her life. A lot of good that had done her.

She was lying on the bed in the same frilly little girl's room, her vision dim. And the same man was standing over her. The man with the black hood. Only this time, as he stood over his victim, he reached for the hem of the head covering.

The part of him that was still Ben Walker held his breath. *Take it off. Take it off.* He chanted in his mind. For a heart-stopping moment, the man hesitated, his hand trembling.

Then he grabbed the bottom and pulled the hood over his head.

Ben's breath caught as he saw the face through the victim's dimming vision.

He had only a momentary glimpse, but he was sure he recognized the person. Strange as it seemed.

The figure bent down and tenderly pressed a kiss on the woman's cheek.

Jesus. Ben gasped. He had to tell Cole and Judd what he'd seen.

Only when he tried to claw his way back to his real self—to Ben Walker's body—he was plunged into absolute blackness where nothing existed besides his consciousness.

Help me, he called out.

Nobody answered, because nobody could hear him.

He was totally and utterly alone.

Sage. He called to her, even when he knew she couldn't hear him. *Sage.*

CHAPTER SEVENTEEN

From far away, Ben heard someone shouting his name. Hope leaped inside him.

"Sage?" he whispered.

"No. It's me. Cole. Ben, wake up."

Strong hands shook him. Disappointment surged through him. It wasn't Sage.

"Ben! Wake up."

He struggled to obey but couldn't do it until he felt a hard slap across his face.

An eternity passed before his eyes blinked open.

"Thank God," Cole breathed.

He and Chief Judd were both on their haunches, staring down at him.

"What happened?" Judd asked.

"I . . ." He stopped and glanced at Cole, then back at the chief again. "I got inside the dead woman's memories."

The chief swore. "Is this some kind of joke?"

"No joke. And I know who the killer is."

Laurel shifted on the bed. "I wish I could help you dig that thing out of the wall."

"You're stuck over there," Sage said as she glanced up at

her sister, then started picking at the bolt again, twisting the fork to scrape off more plaster.

"How long does he leave you alone?"

"For hours. I'm not exactly sure. But he's gone more than he's here."

Sage cleared her throat. "Laurel, I'm sorry I abandoned you."

"What do you mean?"

"I mean, I stopped coming back to town because I hated dealing with Mom. I felt different on my own, and I didn't want to sink back into the relationship we had."

"I understand."

"I should have been there for you."

"You were my role model. I was doing what you said I should. Studying hard so I could make something of myself the way you did. I was so proud of you, and I wanted that, too."

"Did the two of you really have a fight at the Crab Shack?"

Laurel made a low sound. "Yes. She came in and started yelling at me."

"The chief said it was about your grades. I checked with the college, and as far as I could tell, your grades were fine."

"No. It was actually about money. She wanted me to give her more of what I was making at work. I mean, she came down there to see if she could get my check before Bettie gave it to me. You know she's always short of cash."

"She shouldn't be taking it from you."

"She says I should be paying her rent."

"Give me a break."

Laurel sucked in a breath and let it out. "There's something I keep thinking about. The guy who's got me knows about the fight. He said he'd be a better parent to me than Mom."

Sage had been working while they talked. Now she looked up.

"Bettie overheard the fight," she said. "She told us it was over your grades. Maybe she told that to the chief, too. And that's what everyone thought."

"I guess," Laurel mused aloud. "She was real sympathetic afterwards. I guess she told the guy about it. The guy who kidnapped me."

"Or she did it for him. Like she did with me."

"He wants me for his little girl," Laurel said. "He kept telling me how great it would be, but he doesn't seem any better at it than Mom." She waited a beat, then said, "He wants me to tell him he's a good parent. But then when I do, he says that I'm just saying what he wants to hear. It's scary, the way he can't make up his mind."

"Or he's too volatile to keep anything good going."

Sage went back to work. Once she'd gotten started, it was easier to dig into the wall. She broke through a layer of plaster and thought she might be able to pull the chain free. But when she yanked on it, she realized that the thing was screwed into a piece of wood.

Tears welled in her eyes, and she turned her head away from her sister.

"Sage?"

She didn't answer. It seemed like she'd been working for hours, and she'd gotten exactly nowhere. Well, maybe not quite. As she jabbed at the wood with the fork, she saw that it was rotted. Maybe she could get the bolt loose, after all. And then what?

"What are you saying—that you did a séance out here?" Chief Judd made a snorting sound. "You expect me to believe you're connecting with the spirit world? That's what coming to my house and saying you needed my help was all about?"

Ben closed his eyes again, silently asking for the strength to keep himself from lunging at the jerk. Well, maybe that wasn't fair. What were the chances he would have believed what he'd done was possible if he hadn't experienced it himself?

When he opened his eyes again, he focused on the chief. "We don't have a lot of time, so let me give you the short version of why I can do it. I was shot during a narcotics raid and had one of those near-death experiences you've heard about. I mean with my consciousness hovering in the air, looking down at Ben Walker lying on a table in the emergency room. As you may have noticed, I came back to myself. And since then, I've found that when I touch a dead person, I get their last memories. Not a skill I'd wish on anyone. But it does come in handy on occasion. Until I came to Doncaster, I'd only used it with the recently dead." He laughed mirthlessly. "The quick in and out. But somehow, with these women who had been dead for months, I have trouble fighting my way back to myself."

He kept his gaze on Judd. "I came out here because I thought I could learn something about the kidnapper. I think I have."

He struggled to a sitting position. "Last time, when I got into the other woman's memories at the warehouse, her captor was with her when she died, but I could only see a person whose head was covered by a black hood. This time, I saw the person's face.

"Are you going to tell me it was one of the men who run this town?" Judd demanded.

"No. I'm going to tell you it was Bettie Henderson."

"What? I thought it was a guy."

202

"So did we. I guess that's what Bettie wanted her victims to think. But when the guy took off the hood, I saw her standing there big as life."

"How could she pull that off?"

Ben thought about it. "It was Bettie, but she didn't look like herself. She was more masculine. Like she really was a man. Bettie's twin if she had a brother."

"Weird," Judd mused aloud.

Cole's gaze narrowed. "What if she's got one of those split personalities? You know, another person inside her body."

"Come on," Judd said, incredulous.

"You have a better explanation?" Cole asked.

"No. But I don't believe this one," the chief said. He turned to Ben. "And I don't believe that you had some kind of vision and decided there was a reason Bettie Henderson has been running around in a black hood kidnapping girls."

Before Ben could say anything, the chief continued. "You met her at the restaurant, right?"

"Of course. How else would I know who she was?"

"I think this whole thing is bull. What are you going to tell me about this guy?" he gestured toward Cole, "That he used some kind of mumbo jumbo to find the body? Or did you all plant it here?"

"Why the hell would we do that?" Ben asked.

"To sucker me into something."

"Think what you like." Ben got to his feet. "All I want to do is find Sage and Laurel. And you've got another murder victim on your hands. She's probably the other girl who disappeared last year. Take care of her while we go after Bettie Henderson. If I'm wrong, we're no worse off than we were before I had that vision you're sneering at. But remember, you've been losing women in town for the past five years, and you have no damn idea who's doing it."

203

They glared at each other. When the chief looked away, Ben gave it one more try.

"Is Bettie from around here, and if not, do you happen to know how long she's been in town?"

Judd considered the question. "Seems like she's been here five or six years. I think she arrived around the same time I did."

"And what else do you know about her?"

"Not a lot. She did her job and didn't give me any trouble." He thought for a moment. "But I did hear that she could be hard on the girls who worked for her. Sometimes she was nice as pie, and other times she was a holy terror."

Judd dragged in a breath and let it out. Ben could see that something was bothering the chief.

"What is it?" he asked.

"The girls started disappearing about the time she arrived in Doncaster." He kept his gaze on Ben. "Okay, for now, what if we go with your vision?"

"Thank you."

"It's the only lead we've got."

Ben didn't point out that there might be a better lead if the man had taken Laurel's kidnapping seriously.

"I've got a computer in my truck," the chief said. "I can look up her address."

They hurried back to the truck. Ben sat in the front seat, and Cole stood on the driver's side of the truck while the chief typed in the information.

"She's got an apartment in town."

"Doesn't sound like a very good place to hold anyone captive," Ben said.

"Yeah. Wait a minute. It looks like she inherited a piece of property from an uncle at 629 Waverly Road. It's outside of town. On a five-acre lot."

Ben sat up. "That's more like it."

He was still staring at the screen. "It says here she spent time in Spring Grove."

"A state mental hospital?"

"Right."

"Christ. What else do you have?."

"It says she was married to someone named Jim Terry."

"I'd like to know more, but we don't have time to fool around." He turned to Cole. "We've got to move."

Sage gave a mighty tug, and the bolt came free of the wall, slapping the chain against the floor.

She gathered up the metal links and rushed across the room to Laurel. The two sisters hugged each other tightly.

"You did it."

"Yeah. I guess he was in too much of a hurry to make sure this thing was entirely secure."

"Or he never figured you'd keep working to dig it out."

"Now we've got to figure out how to get out of this room. There must be a way, or he wouldn't have us chained up."

"Or it's an extra precaution."

Still holding the chain, she crossed the room and tried the door. It was locked. Next she ran to the window and pulled the curtains aside. Behind the glass, she could see boards nailed across the opening from the outside and daylight filtering through "I can break the glass." Sage swung the chain at the window, shattering several panes.

"Don't cut yourself."

"Give me a pillowcase."

Laurel pulled the case off one of the pillows and tossed it to Sage, who wrapped her hand in the fabric and started pulling out more of the glass. When she'd removed enough, she reached through and pounded at the board.

"It's not tight. I think I can get it off."

She had been working at the boards for a few minutes when they heard a door open and footsteps crossing the wooden floor.

"Mr. Hood is back," Laurel sobbed. "What are we going to do now?"

Sage sprinted back to where she'd been sitting on the floor, pushing the chair in front of the place where she'd pulled the bolt from the wall.

She lay down and closed her eyes as though she was still sleeping off the dose of chloroform or whatever Bettie Henderson had given her. But her eyes were slitted as she watched the hooded man walk into the room. She could tell from his body language that he was angry.

As she stared at him, she wasn't able to think of him as anything but a monster.

"I tried," he shouted. "I tried so hard, but you wouldn't go along with me."

Laurel stared at him. "I tried, too. But it was hard to know what you wanted."

"Just a loving little girl."

"I am a loving little girl."

He made a snorting sound. "Don't give me that crap. You sure as hell don't sound like it."

CHAPTER EIGHTEEN

"How far is it from here?" Ben asked the chief, struggling to keep the panic out of his voice.

"Three miles."

"Hurry. There might not be much time left."

Ben leaped out of the truck. He and Cole ran to the car. As the truck pulled away, they followed. When they reached the main road, they turned left and sped away from Doncaster. As they rounded a curve, a flashing red and blue light made the chief slam on his brakes.

Four cars had piled up, their mangled frames blocking both lanes. A couple of men and women stood on the shoulder, and another was lying on the ground near one of the cars.

Two police cruisers had pulled up at the scene. Ben could see an officer directing traffic. Another was talking to one of the men standing by the road.

Hadn't Judd heard about the accident on the radio? Maybe, but there must not be any other way to get to Bettie's house.

Judd jumped out of his truck and hurried toward one of the officers. As Ben watched them talking, he wanted to run up and say they were on an emergency mission, and they had to get past this mess. But he stayed where he was. He had no creds in this town, but if anyone could get them moving again, it was the chief of police.

Ben could hear the wail of an ambulance in the distance. Christ, more emergency vehicles to block the road.

He brought himself up short. If ambulances were coming, someone was hurt. But he didn't know them. He knew Sage. He loved Sage, and if anything happened to her, he didn't know how he would go on.

That realization slammed into him. He loved her! He had to find her. Before it was too late.

Judd ran back to the truck and called to them. "Follow me."

He maneuvered the vehicle onto the shoulder, inching past a mangled car. Ben followed, drawing a dirty look from the middle-aged woman driver.

Ignoring her, he pushed past, then breathed out a sigh as they swung back onto the blacktop and sped up.

Judd led them to the outskirts of town, then stopped along the road.

Up a gravel driveway, Ben could see an old Victorian that would have been memorable if it were in good repair.

In front of it was parked what looked like a ten-year-old Ford.

Judd drew his weapon as they hurried up the drive.

Clad in the black hood, the monster swung around and glared at Sage. "It was working this time. It was finally working."

Sage doubted it. He'd killed at least four other women. But she knew he must be delusional if he could kidnap women and think he could turn them into his dead daughter.

He kept speaking, addressing Sage now. "You spoiled it

all by coming to Doncaster. Wendy and I would have had a wonderful time together if you hadn't screwed it all up."

She wanted to tell him he was the one who had spoiled it. Whatever "it" was. But she knew that was exactly the wrong tack to take. This man was dangerous, and he obviously had no sense of reality.

She was wracking her brain for some way to handle him when she realized she had run out of time.

He raised his arm, and she saw a gun in his hand. Ben's gun. The one Bettie must have taken from the motel room.

Sage's heart was pounding so hard that she thought it might break through the wall of her chest. Her muscles tensed to the snapping point. She had to force herself to think.

He didn't know that she'd gotten the chain out of the wall. That was her best advantage. Her only advantage.

His gaze flitted around the room, and he lit on the broken glass in the window.

"What the hell happened?"

As he took a step forward, she coiled her whole body, knowing that she had only one chance to get this right.

"This place looks deserted," Cole said as the trio made its way carefully up the driveway.

"Bettie probably doesn't live here," Ben replied. "She probably just uses the house to hold her victims captive."

The discussion was cut short when they heard a shot ring out.

Ben leaped for the front door, kicked it open, and was inside before he knew where he was going.

The house was dark, but he saw light coming from under a door down the hall. He charged in that direction and threw the door open.

Sage was on her knees, facing a figure dressed all in black who had a gun in one hand and the other raised to protect his head as she swung a length of chain. The heavy links flew at the dark-clad man, and he jumped back, cursing.

Then he spotted Ben and turned, aiming the gun toward him.

"No," Sage screamed as the chain swung at the black-hooded figure. He cried out as the heavy links hit him.

Ben sprang forward, bringing the man the ground.

Leaping on top of him, Ben wrenched his gun hand back, as Cole and Chief Judd pounded into the room.

The gun fired again, and Sage rushed forward, stamping on Mr. Hood's wrist. He screamed but held on to the weapon.

Ben bashed the man's head against the floor, and he went still. Judd charged forward and grabbed the gun. Then he whipped out his cuffs and secured the guy's hands behind his back.

When the man was cuffed, Ben reached for Sage. She came into his arms, and they clung together.

She'd held herself together while she'd been a captive. Now she could admit her fear. She'd been terrified that he'd never hold her again.

"Are you all right?" Ben asked, his voice rough with emotion.

"Yes."

"Thank God."

Ben turned toward the young woman on the bed. "You're Laurel?"

"Yes."

"Are you okay?"

"I am now. He was going to kill us. But Sage got the

chain out of the wall, and she used it to hit him just as he fired the gun."

Cole Marshall yanked the hood off their captor's face. He and everyone else in the room stared in astonishment.

The guy lying on the floor looked a little like Bettie Henderson, if Bettie had been a man with slicked-back hair. The features were hard-etched. The eyes angry.

"Get the hell off me," he demanded in a deep voice.

"Not likely," Chief Judd answered as he kept his gaze on the guy. "Who are you?"

"Jim Terry."

"The hell you say."

"Don't take Wendy away from me."

"How many times have you killed Wendy?"

"I would never kill her. I love her so much."

"She was your daughter?"

"Not was. She *is* my daughter. Mine and Bettie's." Something in his eyes changed. "But Bettie got into one of her fits and killed her."

"What?" Sage gasped.

"We covered it up. We made it look like an accident."

"And what happened to Jim Terry?" the chief prodded.

"He died," the figure on the floor sobbed out.

As Sage watched, the masculine features softened, and she saw Bettie. For a moment she looked like herself. Then her face changed again. "That's wrong. Jim Terry didn't die. I couldn't let him. Not after everything we've been through. He's right here."

Tears filled Bettie's eyes. "I just wanted Wendy back," she said in a quavery voice.

The police chief began to speak. "So you kidnapped girls. And when it didn't work out, you killed them."

"Jim did it." This time Bettie seemed to be speaking.

"I don't want to hear anymore of this crap," Chief Judd growled. Then he began again, "You have the right to remain silent. . ." When he'd finished reading Bettie her rights, the chief pulled out his cell phone and called the station house. "I want a patrol car at 629 Waverly Road."

Sage looked back at her sister. "Laurel is still chained to the bed," she told the chief.

Judd walked over and examined the place where Laurel's chain was attached to the wall. "I've got some tools in the truck." He handed his weapon to Ben. "I'll be right back. Keep her covered."

Ben trained the chief's gun on Bettie, but it was clear that the fight had gone out of her.

Judd was back in a few minutes carrying a toolbox. From it he took a bolt cutter and severed the chain. Then he carefully cut the cuffs off of both women. Laurel flexed her arm, looking at the place where she'd been manacled.

"I thought I was never getting out of here alive," she murmured.

Sage crossed to her, and they hugged.

"Thank you. Thanks to all of you."

Chief Judd helped Bettie to her feet and hustled her out of the room.

When the rest of them came outside, a patrol car had already taken Bettie away.

"I'm ordering a psych eval for her," Judd said to the group. "She's one mixed-up individual. Ben kept his gaze on the chief. "And what about the smuggling operation?"

I'm turning that over to the State Police—assuming you were serious about getting me access to that lawyer."

"Yes. We can discuss that later today. Right now, I'd like you to call ahead and tell the hospital that Laurel is coming in for a checkup."

The chief made the call, and Cole drove them to the hospital, where the staff took her right away.

After Laurel had disappeared into the back, Sage glanced at Ben, but he looked more closed up than she'd ever seen him. He'd embraced her when he found her. Now he looked like he wanted to be anywhere but with her. They needed to talk, but that was going to have to wait until Laurel was settled.

When she emerged with a clean bill of health an hour later, they headed for the Baker house where Laurel packed some clothes. From there they drove to the motel where Ben and Sage had been staying. After their heartfelt thanks, Cole left for Baltimore, and Sage turned to her sister.

Ben watched the sisters disappear into the unit they'd originally booked for Sage. He stood looking at the closed door for long moments, then went back to the room where he and Sage had been staying, the room where he had given in to his feelings for her. Later, when he'd known a serial killer had her, he'd been terrified that he couldn't save her life.

Thank God he'd been able to rescue her in time. But now what? Even if he loved her, nothing fundamental had changed. He was still the man who had worked as the security chief on the *Windward*. He was still the man who had let people die. The man who knew he should be punished for his sins.

Maybe it would be better if he packed up his stuff now and went back to Baltimore. He could send someone from Decorah down for Sage and Laurel.

He clenched his teeth. He'd been a lot of things, but coward wasn't one of them. He'd wait for her, and . . .

That thought and his breath choked off as the key turned

in the lock and Sage stepped into the room.

The only thing he could think to say to her was, "How's your sister?"

"Better than you might expect. She's not going to live with Mom. We talked about transferring her credits to The University of Maryland, Baltimore County."

"What's your mom going to do?"

"The same as always, I assume. That's not my concern," she clipped out.

"Is Laurel going to live with you?"

"That depends."

"On what?"

"What she and I work out."

She stood by the door, and he thought she might explain what she meant. Instead, she said, "I didn't thank you for everything you did. How did you find us?"

"Cole located the other body, and I touched it the way I did at the warehouse."

"Andrea Dvorak?"

"I assume so."

"How did he find her?"

"He's got a sense of smell that's almost superhuman. That's how he knew you'd left here in a car. And that someone had anesthetized you."

"What did you see when you touched Andrea?"

"I saw the man take off his black hood, and I saw Bettie's face."

"She took off the hood?"

"Yes. When Andrea was dying. To kiss her good-bye. Chief Judd didn't want to believe how I'd gotten any new information, but I made him help us locate the house Bettie had inherited from her uncle."

"Thank you," she breathed.

She shifted her weight from one foot to the other.

"No thanks necessary. I was doing my job."

"Your job. And was touching Andrea as bad as touching Magdalina?"

He gave a little nod.

"I wasn't there to pull you back."

"Cole did it."

"Thank God." She swallowed hard. "I think you went above and beyond on this assignment."

"I . . . had to find you," he answered, hearing the emotion in his voice.

"Thank you for telling me all that." Sage clenched and unclenched her fists, seeing the closed expression in Ben's eyes. Figuring she had nothing to lose—or everything—she said, "But we need to talk about us."

"That's pretty direct."

"I think I have to be."

She could see him stiffen and knew that in the next few moments everything would change—for the better or they would get much worse. She almost wished she'd kept her mouth shut. Then she forced herself to plunge ahead.

"You had a dream about me, where we were on that ship together."

"The *Windward*," he interjected.

"You said I was punishing you for what you'd done there, and that . . . uh. . . I had you in my power."

He nodded tightly.

"I just went through a terrible experience, where a killer had me in his power. I was terrified of what he—I thought he was a man—was going to do. I worked like mad to free myself before he could come back and . . . kill me and Laurel." She felt her chest tighten as she said it.

"Like the slaves on the *Windward*," he muttered.

"No. Not exactly. They were there because they wanted to be. They didn't realize they might be risking their lives."

He shifted on the bed. "I guess that's right."

"Putting yourself in someone's power voluntarily is different from having the choice taken away."

"What does that have to do with what we're talking about?"

"You keep beating yourself up for what you've done. I want you to see that I trust you completely. And I want you to understand that you trust yourself."

She saw his confusion, and she pressed ahead before she lost her nerve. "Tie me to the bed. Naked. Like you were tied down in that dream you keep thinking about. Then do whatever you want to me. Find out what you're really like in that kind of situation."

Disbelief bloomed on his face. "You're kidding, right?"

"Are you afraid to try it?" she demanded.

"No!"

"Good. Because I'm not." She made her voice businesslike, when she was so nervous she felt light-headed. "I guess we should strip the covers off the bed."

He kept his gaze on her as he stood up. She moved to the other side, and they pulled the spread, blanket and top sheet off the end of the bed. She looked at the mattress, finding two handles on each side. Pointing them out, she said, "We can use those to tie me down."

"And what do we use for rope?"

She laughed. "We can rip up the top sheet—and leave some money to pay for it."

He thought for a moment. "I guess I've got something in my car we can use."

He walked to the door and exited the room, and she wondered if he was going to drive away or come back. He reappeared a minute later with a roll of duct tape, his expression challenging.

Her mouth was dry as she looked at the tape, but she managed to say, "You're in charge. Tell me what you want me to do."

He waited so long to answer that she thought he still might back out.

Finally he said, "Take off your clothes and lie down on the bed."

Was he testing her to see if she'd go through with it? Her hands weren't quite steady as she pulled off her tee shirt and bra, then unhooked and unzipped her jeans. When she was naked, she lay down on the bed with a pillow behind her head. She had never done anything like this in her life, and she felt a strange mixture of fear and sexual excitement.

He stood over her, looking down at her body, his eyes bright. "Stretch out your arms and legs to the side."

She did as he asked, already feeling more vulnerable. And the feeling increased as he wrapped her right wrist with the tape, then attached the other end to the handle on the side of the mattress.

"Okay?" he asked.

"Yes," she managed to say.

He swiftly did the same with other hand, then went on to do her ankles.

A little trickle of fear made her shiver as she moved her arms and legs as far as the tape would allow. Maybe she could have ripped herself free, but she didn't want to do it. She wanted to find out what would happen.

He stayed where he was as he pulled off his shirt and tossed it away, and she stared at his broad chest with the scar angling through the dark hair. He kept his jeans on, but she could see from the bulge at the front of his fly that this was exciting him.

Her throat was so dry that she could barely speak, but she managed to say, "You'd better tape my mouth."

"Why?"

"So you have complete control over me."

"What are you doing, topping from the bottom?"

"That's an expression you learned on the *Windward*?"

"Yeah."

"An interesting way to put it. But go ahead and do it."

His manner was grim as he pulled off one more piece of tape and pressed it over her mouth, making her nerves jump. What if he went too far? Could she get out a scream?

He took the other pillow from the head of the bed, raising her hips with a hand under her butt, and arranged the pillow so that her middle was thrust upward toward him, giving him total access to the most vulnerable part of her body.

He was frightening her and exciting her at the same time. She could feel wetness gathering between her legs. He touched her there, running a finger through the folds of her sex, collecting some of the slick moisture, then wiping his finger on her abdomen.

He could whip her now. For that matter he could take out a knife and cut her. Instead he sat down on the side of the bed and stroked her cheek, then her collarbone, working his way downward to her breasts, lifting and shaping them in his hands, making her nipples rise to tight peaks. He skimmed the very tips with his fingers, then took them between his thumbs and fingers, twisting and pulling on them, increasing her arousal so that she had trouble lying still.

Leaning over, he replaced one of his hands with his mouth, sucking on her, taking her nipple between his teeth, teasing her with small bites that alternated with the sucking motion, drawing a moan from her gagged mouth.

He raised his gaze to her face as he slid his free hand down her body, making a trip through her wet, swollen folds and pressing his finger into her vagina, slipping in and out, imitating the motion of intercourse.

She raised her hips toward him, silently pleading with him to stroke her clit. She was sure he knew what she wanted, but he ignored the plea.

He moved away from her, and she wanted to scream in frustration. Then she saw that he was standing up so that he could unbutton and unzip his jeans. He pulled them off, along with his briefs, freeing an enormous erection, and she knew this was turning him on as much as it was arousing her.

Leaning down, he played with her breasts again, making her writhe on the bed in frustration. Then he knelt between her legs and spread the lips of her sex, exposing her to his gaze.

"Lord, that's a beautiful sight," he murmured, slipping one finger into her again, twisting it with a maddening circular motion. "You're all hot and creamy for me."

She couldn't speak, but she hoped her eyes told him how much she needed release.

He smiled down at her. "You're right. Having you in my power is a learning experience."

Gently, he stroked a hand up and down her ribs, then caressed her abdomen and ran his fingers through her pubic hair. Although his touch was light, she was so sensitized now that she felt like she might burst.

He continued speaking. "Do you need to come?"

She nodded and rocked her hips against the pillow.

"I could free one of your hands so you could show me what you do when you pleasure yourself. Would you do that for me?"

Her face reddened, the thought of doing something so personal in front of him filling her with embarrassment. But she nodded again.

"But I'd rather do this," he said, kneeling between her legs

Lowering his head, he lapped at her with his tongue, slipping his finger into her again, stroking in and out as he sucked on her clit then caressed it with his tongue. Small tremors shuddered through her sex, tremors he must feel. He continued to work her with his mouth, bringing her up and up until an all-consuming climax rocketed through her.

While she was still coming, he shifted his position and plunged his cock into her, moving in a frantic rhythm, following her over the edge after only a few quick strokes.

He cried out, gathering her in his arms, and she yanked one of her wrists free so that she could pull the tape off her mouth, then circle his shoulder with her arm and hold him close.

He lowered his lips to hers for a long, hungry kiss.

"That's what you wanted to do when you had me in your power?" she gasped when he raised his head. "Make me so hot I thought I was going to explode."

"Yes."

"I think it's a good sign."

He laughed, then sat up and twisted around so that he could untape her legs while she pulled her other hand free.

He came down beside her, holding her.

"You learned something about yourself?" she asked.

"Yeah."

"And you're okay with what you found out?"

"Yes."

"What was it?"

"That . . . I'm the same as I was before the *Windward*. Well, more aware of the dark side of life, but the same man."

"Good." She swallowed. "I realized something about myself, too. Not just then, but as we got to know each other. I've had relationships before, and they never worked out. I think a lot of it was my fault. I was afraid to open myself totally to a man because deep down I was terrified of being dependent—like Mom."

"You're not her."

"I know. But she was a lousy role model. Then I met you, and I knew everything could be different for me—if I stopped being afraid to open myself up." She dragged in a breath and let it out. "Maybe I was testing myself too. Seeing how far I could open up to you."

She found his hand and knitted her fingers with his. "Ben, I know there are people who would say we only met a few days ago, and we should wait to . . . decide where we want to go from here."

She felt him relax and knew she was giving him the reassurance that he needed, and perhaps she needed too.

"Promise me you'll give us a chance."

He swallowed hard. "I can do that."

She rolled toward him, pillowing her cheek on his shoulder and holding on to him. "And I want you to know, I accept everything you are. Even the ghost stuff—or do you want to stop getting memories from the dead?"

He shook his head. "I'd like to stop, but if I can help people, I will."

She held him even tighter. "If you want me there with you when you do it, I will be."

"You'd do that?"

"Of course." That and so much more. But now she knew they had time to find out how much the two of them were going to mean to each other.

She wanted to tell him she loved him. But she wasn't sure he was ready to hear that yet. Instead she snuggled against him. She knew that he still had doubts about himself, but she was here beside him now, and she knew that as long as they were together, they'd manage anything the future threw at them.

PRAISE FOR REBECCA YORK

Rebecca York delivers page-turning suspense.
—Nora Roberts

Rebecca York never fails to deliver. Her strong characterizations, imaginative plots and sensuous love scenes have made fans of thousands of romance, romantic suspense and thriller readers.
—Chassie West

Rebecca York will thrill you with romance, kill you with danger and chill you with the supernatural.
—Patricia Rosemoor

(Rebecca York) is a real luminary of contemporary series romance
—Michael Dirda, The Washington Post Book World

Rebecca York's writing is fast-paced, suspenseful, and loaded with tension.
—Jayne Ann Krentz

ABOUT REBECCA YORK

A USA Today Best-Selling Author, Rebecca York is a 2011 recipient of the Romance Writers of America Centennial Award. Her career has focused on romantic suspense, often with paranormal elements.

Her 16 Berkley books and novellas include her nine-book werewolf "Moon" series. KILLING MOON was a launch book for the Berkley Sensation imprint. She has written 52 books for Harlequin Intrigue, many in her popular 43 Light Street series. She has written for Harlequin, Berkley, Dell, Tor, Carina Press, and Pageant Books.

Her many awards include two Rita finalist books. She has two Career Achievement awards from Romantic Times: for Series Romantic Suspense and for Series Romantic Mystery. And her Peregrine Connection series won a Lifetime Achievement Award for Romantic Suspense Series.

Many of her novels have been nominated for or won RT Reviewers Choice awards. In addition, she has won a Prism Award, several New Jersey Romance Writers Golden Leaf awards and numerous other chapter awards.

Web site: http://www.RebeccaYork.com
Facebook: Ruth Glick
Twitter: rebeccayork43

BOOKS BY REBECCA YORK:
http://rebeccayork.com/the-books/complete-book-list/